I0566131

HEART LAND

Silky Oak Press
for books that love you back

This first edition published 2015 by Silky Oak Press
www.silkyoakpress.com.au
ABN 45 969 162 506

Copyright © D.B. Allen 2014
ISBN: 978 0 9923928 4 0

All rights reserved. No part of this publication may be reproduced,
stored in a retrieval system, or transmitted in any form or by any
means, electronic, mechanical, photocopying, recording or otherwise,
without the prior written consent of the publisher.

The characters and events in this book are fictitious. Any similarity to real
persons, living or dead, is coincidental and not intended by the author.

Written by DB
Edited by Greg
Proofread by Greg
Book Design by Ron
Cover Design by Juliette
All Illustrations by the Author

This book was written in American English
and typeset in Adobe Garamond Pro 12/17

Silky Oak Press

HEARTLAND

D.B. Allen

For Mark Tredinnick
and words that find heart in a landscape

There are threads running through this series of stories. Connection of people and places and events. You might like to actively search for these, or you might prefer to let them find you. The choice, as the reader, is yours.

DB Allen.

LAST STORM ... FIRST

IT WAS JUST BEFORE FIVE WHEN JOHN McLEAN FIRST noticed the color of the afternoon. He parked his truck on a rise on Route 281, watched the grass rolling silvery-green towards an irascible sky. John was never a man to loiter, but even in those brief minutes the clouds grew noticeably darker. A burgeoning mélange of water, air and earth — spiraling and spinning and twisting. Between the darkest cloudbanks the sky was glacial green, grey curtains draped over a horizon that was a dirty, burning orange. Lightning flashed searchlights through folds of cloud, now layered one-on-another, like waxen corpses. Distant thunder rumbled, burrowing through earth and rising up through the seat of a lonely red pickup truck.

John McLean was local. Born and bred. A God-fearing man. It was real late in the season, but he knew that sky meant trouble. He just hoped God was watching...

The first hailstones were ball-peening the hood as John stopped his truck out back of the family home in

Winifred, Oklahoma. He hurried inside, started yelling for everyone to get out to the bunker. He sprinted from room to room, unsure who was home and who wasn't. Mabel was in the kitchen fixing supper, little Sue-Ellen close by and begging to help. Joshua was in his room with his best friend Jeb Walker; crossed-legged arguments over baseball cards. Jeb's folks lived over at Blackthorn. Thirty miles. No time to take him home, so the boy'd have to stay. That meant there'd be five, sheltering in a bunker built for four. Not so comfortable, but at least everyone would be safe. And kids didn't take up much space.

The first twister was touching ground as they ran for the storm bunker. A second was roping between cloud banks. Claws of wind tore at their hair and their clothes. The rain and hail dealt icy stings to the skin. Late season and so cold. The thunder felt like it could lift dirt clear from the earth. They could hear roaring from across the prairie. A thousand engines? A million stamping hooves? Dark columns of rain and dirt and debris spinning beneath the belly of the clouds, like the spawn of some apocalyptic beast.

It was hard to be brave ... when you were so scared.

The bunker door was made from plates of steel originally slated for USS Kentucky. Heavy and grey. Rust and rivets like acne. When John McLean built something, he built it to last. The storm bunker took him two years. It wasn't just the steel door. The bunker had been dug into the side of an earth berm, with double concrete walls, circular and reinforced with steel beams, sunk forty feet down into the earth. There was plenty of neighborly laughter. Winifred had never seen a direct hit. Lucky town. Blessed town. Or maybe Jumpin' John was expecting the Ruskies to drop the big one?

"Raise your glasses boys. Here's cheers ... to the town pessimist."

No one would be laughing now. Not with the color of that sky. There was a first storm for every town. As he struggled to pull the immense door closed, John caught a last glimpse of the horizon. He counted five twisters touching down.

'Five...'

With everyone inside, John worked ten inch-thick bolts across the door and into holes running deep in the bunker walls. He'd set aside rolls of lead flashing to tamp into the gaps around the door, but he'd been using his panel mallet today and it was still in the truck. Too late to go out again. Too dangerous. He could hear the sound of tearing leaves. It was close now. Perhaps it was a good time to pray.

'Our Father, who art in heaven...'

And the noise only grew louder.

Even through reinforced concrete and battlewagon steel, you could hear the passage of hell outside. The door began to judder; growling and moaning; water like steam, spitting through the cracks. John reached forward, slapped the switch on top of his battery-powered lamp. He saw the faces of his family—citric-colored, and scared. The Walker kid was crying.

'We'll be OK,' he yelled, loud, so they could hear him over the tumult. 'Not even the A-bomb could break through one of my bunkers.'

They stayed in that bunker for hours, waiting for one twister to pass, only to have another arrive, and then another. Finally, when world grew silent and light began to shine chromatic around the gaps in the door, John knew it was safe to open up. The door has shifted on its hinges. Steel built to survive high explosives, now bent and battered by air and water. It was hard to slide back the bracing bolts. The door refused to properly open. John gave it his boot, and again, until eventually, he was able to slide through a gap. He lurched outside, into an apocalypse.

John McLean had served in Korea; did a year with Assistance Command in Vietnam before he finally got out. He'd seen towns and villages razed to stick and ash…

'Oh my Lord.'

...and now his town had vanished. There was not a tree left standing. Not a house. Not a vehicle. It was like a giant broom had reached down and swept the land clean. The McLean family once had a home. They used to have a big attic, yellow walls, white wood-work and a red stone chimney. They were left with a muddy concrete slab and a clear view over the western horizon. The big old elm that once shaded their back porch — maybe a hundred years old — was kindling. John's truck was gone.

Everything ... gone ...

Out to the east, the sky was still black and roaring. Distant walls of debris like trash mountains.

'How many?' he whispered. 'Heavenly Father, how many will there be?'

'Daddy?' a little voice said behind him.

Of course, it was Sue-Ellen. Cheeky little monkey. She'd followed him outside. She was five years old and fearless.

'It's bad, ain't it Daddy?'

John nodded. Her soft fingers touched his. He looked down and saw her beautiful little face, now shining gold in the last light of sunset. She gave him her brave smile.

'Daddy, I think it's OK for us to cry ... y'know ... if we want to.'

That was when reality started jabbing John McLean's heart. It wouldn't let up. As he stood there, with his little girl's hand safely resting inside his own, he realized that he'd lost everything, but still had all he needed. His family was with him. All of them. Alive.

'You go back inside and stay with momma,' he said to Sue-Ellen. 'Tell her Daddy's gonna go check on the other folks. Y'know, make sure everyone's OK.'

His little girl made a face, but turned and squeezed herself in through the bunker door again.

John took a deep breath. Where did you start? How? People were hurting. Folks needed help. And to men like John McLean, that's what life was all about.

It was always about other folks.

"THE SWING"
PANEK
RANCH NE

THE SWING

PART 1 — THE BOY WITH THE CROOKED SMILE

MY HUSBAND WAS A WRITER. NOT THAT HE EVER TOLD me. I didn't find out until this week, more than twelve years after he left me, just how much he'd actually written. Turns out he was some kind of writer. He had little more than an Elementary School education.

But that was my husband. He was always surprising me.

And when I took the time to read his words I discovered a self-made man, a journeyman, but a man terribly lost. He sure had come a long way from where his life began. He was resilient and he was resourceful. But he was also fragile. He was heavy-laden with secrets. A complex and deeply-wounded man. He told me his story once — back when I was still little more than a kid myself — back in the days when we used to actually speak with each other.

They christened him Karol Piotr Pedanski. A lonely, quiet little boy. A boy with a crooked smile. I'd only ever seen one childhood photograph. A framed and faded sepia square, showing a fair-haired boy with pot-handled ears. A tabby clawing and squirming from inside his folded arms. That lop-sided smile I came to love, but seldom saw. One photograph…

Karol was born in a grey concrete hospital down near the Gdansk shipyards in Poland. A dark, muted world of rusting green derricks, inch-thick steel and splashing welder's sparks. He'd come a long way from the cobbled streets of his home. Those endless rows of grey concrete panel blocks. He'd come a long way from the home of Solidarity, Lech Walesa and generations of the Pedanski family. His family survived Hitler and then the Communists. He once told me he was the only male of his generation — his mother raised five girls and a boy — so he was the hope for the future of the family. Not that he ever would admit it, but I don't think he could handle the weight of that family name.

In the mid-seventies, Karl quit. The hope for the family line jumped a cargo ship and sailed over the horizon. He told himself he'd never go back to his country of birth. Never be held down by the expectations of others. He wanted to live like his Pappy — his mother's father — Jerzy Kaczynski.

Karl was only fifteen years old when he ran away.

Eventually he found himself in New York City — about as far away from the Gdansk shipyards as a man could go. Sea life wasn't what he'd imagined. He was tired of the terrible living conditions, the loneliness and the abuse — though he would never tell me exactly what they did to him — and so, on a foggy, rat-infested night at the Newark docks, he swung himself down a mooring line and hitched fifteen miles. He crawled right into core of the Big Apple.

Karl evaporated into the coffee-house bohemia of Greenwich Village. He would have been a beautiful young man. Blonde. Quietly handsome. A seventeen year old who told a lot of damn lies. Dodged official-dom. And stayed.

It was the start of the disco era. Studio-54 and designer Cocaine. Down in the Village, Karl discovered new colors. He tried to live a new life. But the free-spirited boy grew into a man who struggled with the burden of living. He became afraid of change, but even more terrified of failure. He never liked standing still for too long. Karl lived inside a permanent tension. He kept reinventing himself. New York City was kind to him like that. Kind, but sometimes cruel.

By the age of twenty five, Karl had lived more life than most men twice his age. He'd done every damn job he could turn his hand to: cab driver, doorman, delivery guy, grocery store Joe; he sold tickets at the Garden, picked up dog shit and mowed grass in Central Park; he even tried bouncer work at a bar on Columbus, but he kept being beaten up by drunks; he'd been twice married.

Karl's first wife worked in a Village bakery. Crystal was a college dropout, in love with the idea of something different. Karl was what she wanted, at least for a while. She was three years older than him. He told me once that she blinded him. A goddess. Venus made flesh. She seemed so grown up. A real woman. They married in the Borough Hall in Queens. The bride wore black.

His second wife was the antithesis to his first. Melanie was an introverted heiress to Wall Street brokerage money. She didn't know what she wanted. Until she met Karl. He told her folks he stemmed from European royalty. They held a society wedding in Manhattan. But the novelty of Karl didn't last. Both of his marriages failed within a year.

Karl refused to let those set-backs slow him down. He kept up the reinvention. He tried all those different careers. He was always successful for a while, until life would swing and things would become too difficult. He'd run again. And then, Karl ran himself out of ideas. He told me how he woke up one morning and wondered what on earth he was going to do next. He was thirty years old. And he'd chewed the Big Apple dry.

With a pocket full of cash from his second divorce, Karl caught an Amtrak to Chicago, and then a second further west. He had vague West Coast ambitions. They were never realized. God only knows why, but he liked the look of Nebraska. Thought it might be the place to start again — so he did. He left the train in Lincoln. It would be his last reinvention.

Ranek was a Polish word for dawn. Karl's Papa Jerzy used the word all the time. It was his way of explaining a fresh start. It became Karl's raison d'etre. He painted the word on a little sign and nailed it to a pair of old white-washed gates up in the far north west of the 'corn-husker' state. The same day he signed the deed papers to what became our ranch. The first day of Karl's eternity.

Ranek Ranch really was a new beginning — in the rolling yellow heart of the New World. And these 122 acres of marginal Nebraska cattle country were going to be his brightest reinvention yet. He'd already lived a charmed life in the U.S. He'd made great things from the opportunities America gave him. He fulfilled the great American ideal — the way a man could flourish, if given the chance to experience freedom. The glossy face of the boy with the crooked smile.

The reality of Karl was much more complex. He

was an idealist. The ranch was part of a romantic notion — of cowboys and campfires and life on the open plains. Karl knew nothing about the mid-west, nothing about Nebraska, and even less about cattle ranching.

He learned the trade quickly. Though he didn't have much formal education, Karl was smart. He listened and he asked the right questions. The other ranchers thought he was goofy. They cut him some slack. So did God. In those early years, the weather was kind to him. Ranek had good rain. Mild winters. Karl was soon making money. The business expanded.

And then it happened again — Karl Pedanski went and got himself married for a third time.

I was a mid-west girl, six years Karl's junior. Another college drop-out that came walking into his life. I was working part-time, trying to save my way to a second shot at a journalism degree. But I was bored with life in the middle of damn nowhere. I was determined that my next school would be one in another state — maybe Arthur Carter at NYU, or Communications at Cornell.

The tall blonde guy with the goof-ball smile was my soul mate — I told myself that as soon as I saw him walk into Darcy's Drug Store in the spring of 1990. I looked into his baby blue eyes and saw something of his heart. The day I met Karl changed my life. Staying in this nameless corner of the Great Plains didn't seem so bad after all. Not if I was staying with Karl.

We had a whirlwind romance, and then a white wedding in Chatfield. It was early fall, 1990. Most folks in the congregation were my friends from town. One of Karl's new rancher buddies supplied a horse and buggy for me to ride up to the church in. My parents gave me away, under sufferance. They told me I was too young to be getting married. Too smart to throw away all that schooling for a life of hard work and child-bearing.

My folks knew something about doing it tough. My dad was a veteran. Korea and Vietnam. He'd moved us all to Nebraska in the seventies after our house was destroyed in an Oklahoma twister. I was a little girl, but I still remember that afternoon. The noise. The way the rain came hissing in through the door of our storm shelter like steam from a boiling pot. Over 500 people died in those storms. We survived thanks to my dad. He and mom were practical people. Heartland born and bred. They got on with life. Survivors. But they were folks who kept to their own. They distrusted foreigners. They never liked Karl. My father had a few too many beers at the wedding, and he told Karl to his face.

Karl and I honeymooned in Vegas. Had ourselves a wild week. All kinds of passion. We would burn up our hotel room one night and be fighting like stray cats the next. When the week was done, we hobbled back to Ranek Ranch. I threw up for a month. Nine months later I gave birth to a little boy. We called him Karl Jnr.

That's what living with Karl was like. Fast-paced. But times were good.

Then came the '93 drought, the storm season of '96. Worst were the wildfires of '99. Karl tried to adapt, and when the losses started to build up, he tried to fight back. But he kept on losing. Soon his Wall Street inheritance was gone. He borrowed against the property — though I never really knew how much — and he started to change.

I can still remember New Year's Eve 1999 — watching a bonfire light up my husband's crooked smile, and thinking that a new century was dawning over Ranek Ranch. It was to be a dark century. Life swung again. And this time, Karl didn't know how to stop it. Things started moving too fast. I lost him — even before the end. What I didn't know was how early he'd lost himself. The stories he told me were only a fraction of who he was. And by the end of 1999, he stopped speaking. He just didn't confide in me anymore.

Oh mercy, I thought I knew my husband. Knew his heartaches and knew his pain. Knew what he wanted from life. Turns out I didn't know anything. Not until I plucked up the courage to go through his stuff.

It took me more than a decade. I was cleaning out the cupboard under the main staircase; that damn awkward triangular room you had to crawl on your hands and knees to get into. It was near the door out to the back porch, so Karl kept his dirty ranch stuff in there. His work boots. One of his rifles. He kept other things in there too. Right at the back of the cupboard, jammed under the stairs, where the cobwebs were heavy with yellow dust, I found the photograph of Karl and the cat, a small jewelry box with a tarnished silver broach, a green steel workers helmet, and a pile of black-covered books. Beautifully bound.

Karl's journals.

What I found that day was a hidden corner of his life. Stories written in a neat hand, to a long lost grandfather. In those baby-blue pages I found a man I scarcely knew. A man terrified of change, but paralyzed at the thought of failure. A man with secrets. A man broken and lost. I plucked up the courage to read his words. Started with his last journal. Wondered how far I'd get…

PART 2 — BROKEN WORDS

Wednesday 23rd August 2000.

I was thinking about you today Papa. And maybe that is the real problem with me — I am always thinking too much. I think too much and then I worry. And my worries weigh me down. On days like today, when I am feeling low, I try to remember the beautiful words in your diaries. The way your words could become color on the page. Words as clear as pictures. The shipyards. Life at sea. Exotic places. I would read your stories of life under iron and steel. Your tales of faraway places and a life of adventure. You set dreams in my heart. You taught me about the beauty of words. That is why I have been writing my books for so long. I want so much to be like you Papa. I wish you were still here.

You were a much better man than my father ever could be. Papa, you left us legacies. Father left wounds. And then, one day, he just left. You taught us to believe in ourselves. I need you today. I need more of you in me. Karl needs to be a man more like Jerzy and less like Piotr. Because another winter is coming. And after the last year of bad weather, I am not so sure we can survive a heavy winter.

I was thinking all these things this afternoon, while I was driving out to the north-west field. I pulled the Blazer off the tire tracks, at the point where the land begins to rise and roll towards the mountain forests of the Panhandle. Even though the weather was warm, I could see winter in the sky. Clouds the color of Gdansk. The Cottonwoods out beyond my fences were just starting to turn lemon-green. Yet, I could still taste summer. Burnt earth on the wind. It got me thinking again — how close the '99 wildfires came.

Under a pair of tired old Juniper trees, my two stud bulls sat together, tail-to-tail, looking like giant red bookmarks. I have told you before Papa, how I named the first bull I bought after you. Well, each beast I have owned since then has been given the same name — and then a number. The two I own these days are Jerzy Two and Six. I had Jerzy Five until last month. His sale kept the bank away from the door for a few weeks. Now I am contemplating selling off his brother. Need to think of a reason to tell Sue-Ellen. Maybe saving for fresh bloodlines or something? She does not need to know about the state of the finances. Anyway, I am sure those bulls knew my thoughts today. Two pairs of brown eyes stared at me suspiciously as I pulled up. And then...

Jerzy Six was always a bit jumpy, ill-tempered and prone to charge a fence or two. He rocked to his feet as soon as I took a step out of the truck. He stamped the straw-colored earth a few times. There were angry licks of yellow dirt. He snorted at me, tossed his head and spun around. That was when I noticed the deep red puncture wounds on his rump. I tried to get closer, but there was no way he would let me. It was getting late. Will have to get to the bottom of this tomorrow morning. Worried!!

Thursday 24th August 2000.

I drove back out to the bulls again this morning. Jerzy Two was in his usual place under the Junipers, but Jerzy Six had moved to the opposite corner of the field. When I drove towards him with the Blazer, he dragged his front legs and charged. He must have only missed the front fender by a few feet. Then he twisted and kicked away, and ran back up towards his friend. I have never seen him so agitated. There were more marks on his rump than yesterday. Cuts and puncture wounds. A lot more.

Originally I suspected he had cut himself on the barbed wire. We had Horn fly again over the summer, but it was nothing the spraying had not controlled. So had I missed another attack? Jerzy Six was a compulsive scratcher. But if we had fly again, why had no other animals been affected? Not one!! A mystery, Papa!!

Must check the cows and yearlings tomorrow. We may need another round of spraying before the fall. More chemicals. More expense.

Friday 25th August 2000.

When I got back from the fields today, all I could do was sit out under the old willow tree behind the house. I do not know why, but I could not go inside. It was like I had been banished from the world of people. I sat on that rope-and-tire swing I made for Karl Jnr a few years back. I sat there for hours. Numb. What I had seen. What I had to do. It was horrible Papa, just horrible. Horn fly was now the least of my problems.

We had lost three yearlings overnight. Three. Two had deep bite marks on the belly and the neck and the face. They were still half alive when I found them. Thrashing on the ground, trying to get back on their feet. Trying to live. But there was no hope. I had to come back to the house to get my big old Winchester. Two shots. Point blank. The volley racing around the patchwork straw hills, before coming back and echoing in my skull. When I opened my eyes again, the thrashing had stopped. There were scarlet rivers on the yellow dust.

Papa, I only had to give the coup-de-grace to those two. The third beast was already like an abattoir scene—bloody skin and bones—most of him had been eaten.

I dragged all three carcasses into a pile, covered them with gas from the truck and set them alight. I did not want coyotes or wild dogs coming around again, creating a nuisance. I watched the orange flames dance. Devil flames. The air was a potpourri, at first heavy with singeing skin and hair, and then there was the summery smell of barbecuing beef. That smell made me feel so guilty…

I kept swinging on Little Karl's tire, staring up towards the hills. Junipers like arrowheads, pointing into a growling red horizon. Fingers of smoke rising. Twenty-five hundred dollars' worth of stock, now smoldering and worthless. A Coyote was yapping in the looming dark. And that was when I started to think about it. No Coyote or wild dog could have done that much damage to a yearling, let alone three. And what about the wounds on Jerzy Six? He was a full-grown Shorthorn bull—over 2,200 pounds—and there were two beasts in that field.

Once it was dark, I went inside. Told Sue-Ellen I was not hungry. Migraine. I went to bed, still putrid and dirty and smelling like smoke. Begged for sleep. But the thoughts would not go away. They would not leave me. So, after Sue came to bed I got myself up.

And now I am writing again. Writing and thinking. Worrying. What the hell sort of animal do we have out there? I keep thinking about the size of those scratch marks on Jerzy Six's rump. How far apart each of those scratch marks were. Huge. I do not mind admitting Papa, I am starting to feel scared.

Saturday 26th August 2000.
I cannot sleep again tonight. Tried watching TV — the NASCARs were running at Bristol — but I could not sit still. Even after I came to bed, and Sue-Ellen offered to do something to help me relax, I was on edge.

Karl Jnr is up with Sue's folks in Chatfield, staying for the weekend. Sue had planned a date night for the two of us. But my heart was not in it. I had not told her about what I had seen in the fields. Told her I was tired from all the work. She understood. But she did not quit easily. She worked me over real good. Still have a wild young wife!! It took me some time to really participate, but she did not give up. I finally found my place. And hers.

Then, after we were done, Sue fell asleep at my side. I lay there, feeling warm and heavy, and I tried to sleep. But all I could do was think about what might be going on outside. What sort of beast might be up there — even at that moment? Papa, what am I going to do about it?

Now I am sitting in the living room. Me and my pen and my journal. Words as therapy. This is how it has been for so long. Since you showed me how, Papa. The evening is quiet. More than quiet. It is like sound now ceases to exist. I lean back in my old leather recliner and stare at the ceiling. Even now, I am imagining all manner of evil creatures, lurking out there in the dark. Maybe they are outside right now. I can almost see them, moving out from the dark forest, their eyes glowing like embers. Glowing like my fear.

Sunday 27th August 2000.

Sue-Ellen drove into town to see her folks and to pick up Little Karl. She likes to go to church with Little Karl when she gets the chance. Says it is important that he learns about right from wrong. Plus her mom was putting on a turkey roast. I know I am not welcome at their house, even if the words are never actually said. Sue-Ellen's mother still will not even talk to me, and her father only opens his mouth to tell me the things I am doing wrong. He fought communists in Korea and Vietnam. Maybe he thinks I am some type of Polish communist? Well Papa, Sue and I do not argue about this one anymore. It is a lost fight.

I drove out to Sandhills to see Debby Clarke, while her Peter was preaching in Rapid City. We did not do much today—just kind of sat and reminisced. I told her about what was happening to my cattle. She told me about her latest date night with that husband of hers. And, once again, I tried to imagine a respectable couple, such as the Clarkes, living a double life like they were.

Debby Clarke sure is a fine woman, Papa. I was reminded of that this afternoon. Fine, like this country. I cannot imagine her ever living in any other place. It is like she was born out of the land. I think she is part of it; the same luxurious sweeps and curves; skin hard-worked and dry, like badlands; eyes as wide and blue as the biggest of big skies. I loved her the first time we met. Still do!!

This afternoon, Debby and I drank iced tea, watching the setting sun make black and gold wave shapes out of the landscape. The time soon got away. Sue-Ellen and Little Karl would be arriving home. I would have to make a detour via the northern gate—to give Sue the illusion I had been working up in the fields. Sue still does not know about Debby. I wonder if I will ever be able to tell her. I do not think I will ever want to. Because, as I sat close to Debby, listening to the metallic grind of the swing seat chains, everything felt right as it was. I did not want to change a thing. And I did not want to go home.

Papa, I know I should feel guilty about that.

Monday 28th August 2000.

Real hot day today. I am sitting out on the porch, enjoying the cooler air. Good old Boss is lying under my feet. Snoring away like a rhinoceros. He sure is an ugly dog, but he would do anything for me. Silly loyal creature!!

I am trying to think of something to write, but the words will not come. Maybe I need to get some sleep. They are saying it will be hot again tomorrow.

Tuesday 29th August 2000.

Summer is refusing to leave without a fight. It came close to one hundred again today. I worked under a gassy, breathless sky. Those Panhandle hills were dark and shivering in the heat. Every time I found myself pointing in the direction of those mountains, I started thinking again about what might be living up there. Can't stop those thoughts. Papa, I am worried.

Sue-Ellen was moody and quiet this evening. She kept giving me the silent back treatment during dinner. She went to bed early. Little Karl started back at school today. The two of us went outside to feed Boss and Aussie. Doors started slamming inside the house.

Does Sue know about Debby Clarke? No. It is not possible. I am sure she thinks I have forgotten what this coming weekend is. Thinks I have forgotten our tenth anniversary. If the truth be told — I did forget last year. Never again. Oh Papa, the yelling!!

Ten years of marriage. Who would have thought I could stick at anything for ten years!! Karl Jnr gave me a concerned look when he heard his mother bawling and hollering. I ruffled his head and smiled. I told him what was happening. Shared my anniversary secret. Not a word to your mother, I told him. He smiled. Understood. He is a smart boy. Gets that from his mom.

After Little Karl went to bed I had a couple of beers and put on some vinyl records. Motown sounds. Then an old *Cream* album. Closed my eyes. It brought back memories of summers in The Village. Those long soulful nights, sitting out with Javier and Juliet; with Marvin Brown, Mister Mulberry and the Cheltenham Twins; drinking Danish beer and listening to sounds, under a choc-fudge sky. The first time I met Crystal was a night like that. I remember she liked the rough skin on my hands ... and where my hands found themselves that same night. I had never felt a naked breast before. I never forgot the divine heaviness. What it was like to kiss skin so soft. Skin that felt like it would melt under your lips.

It is getting hard to write now. Heavy eyes. My fingers are refusing to make the words. I think I will fall asleep smiling tonight. This evening feels like a gift. For the last few hours, I have actually felt good about life.

Wednesday 30th August 2000.
Paralyzed. Feel very low tonight, Papa. Cannot write. Cannot think. The night is so dark.

Thursday 31st August 2000.
I felt better again today. But Sue has been furious. Our anniversary is tomorrow and I have said nothing to her. She has just gone to bed. Now is my chance. I am going to pack a couple of bags—Little Karl already has his stuff packed away—and I will put the reservation letter out on the breakfast table, so she will see it first thing tomorrow.

Ahh, I am sneaky old Karol!!

Saturday 2nd September 2000.
Sue-Ellen is curled up beside me as I write. Snoring. And I thought the guy was supposed to be the one who was sleepy after doing what we just did!!

Remembering our tenth anniversary was a very smart move—even if I had been given the cold-shoulder most of the week, while I was playing dumb. We sure did make up properly tonight. That's twice in two nights. Holiday beds are good for helping folks make up!!

The weekend has been great so far. Better than I expected. We picked up Karl Jnr after school on Friday and left him with Sue's folks in Chatfield. From there, it was only an hour up to South Dakota, Cascades and the same Bed and Breakfast we stayed in on our first anniversary. I even booked the same room. OK, it is not my kind of place—bunny rabbits and lace, lavender bags and pink flowers painted on everything—but Sue loves it and that is the most important thing. We have had a good time so far, but now, as I am writing, I am worried.

I was worried about coming away this weekend. Worried about the ranch. Worried about what might happen while we were away. Those yearlings are worth seven or eight hundred dollars apiece. I cannot afford to lose a single one. But it was our tenth anniversary. I owe Sue big time. I know I have not been easy to live with in recent years. Now, as she lies beside me, and I feel the soft warmth of her skin on mine, and even though I still worry about my ranch, I tell myself I have done the right thing.

Sunday 3rd September 2000.

Home again. Home again and writing. It really was a beautiful day today. Hot and blue. We spent the day down at the river, splashing and swimming and acting like crazy kids. I could not believe we had the swimming hole to ourselves. Can you believe we went skinny dipping? At our age!! We dived and splashed and sat under the waterfalls, letting curtains of silver water splash and dance all around us. Cool and beautiful.

Then something struck me. As we were drying off in the sun, I noticed how beautiful my wife's navel was. I have never noticed it before. Maybe this is because once a man's eyes get down that far on a woman's body, well, they just keep on going down. I mean, it is a crazy thing to notice, but Sue-Ellen has the most perfect little belly-button. Soft and pink and u-shaped. It almost smiles at you. I told her that, and she laughed so hard she started snorting. We both did. It felt so good to laugh. It is just as well we were down at that swimming hole alone — considering what we did next!! I am sure doing that sort of thing is illegal in South Dakota.

It was night by the time we picked up Little Karl in Chatfield, and we drove home in the dark. Headlights started picking up the white lines of Route 385, every bug within a hundred miles of our truck, and glowing fox eyes lurking in the grass beside the road. It made me wish we had come back while it was still light. I do not like glowing eyes.

As we drove into the gates of the ranch, I could feel my mood swinging again. Happiness smothered by the darkness, like the world beyond the Blazer. This was the world to which I was returning. The world I am back inside again. Or maybe this time things will be better. Please Papa, tell me things will be better from now on.

Monday 4th September 2000.

Labor Day holiday today, but there has been no holiday on Ranek Ranch. There is too much work to be done. Too much fencing to repair. Drainage to dig. Phone calls to answer.

Debby Clarke called this morning. She caught me just as I was heading out the back door. Sounded really upset. I had never heard her sound like that. I told her I would call her from the truck. When Sue-Ellen asked me who was on the phone, I told her it was a wrong number. Feel so bad about lying to her.

Debby and Peter had been fighting. A really big argument. Maybe the biggest they had ever had. She told Peter she did not want to go on living a double life—churching with her husband on Sunday after those date nights. The swinging with strangers. It was all so murky and disgusting—a man of God and adulterous sex. She told me Peter knew what he was doing was wrong. She wanted him to stop, before someone found out and her husband's reputation was ruined. But he could not stop himself. He refused to talk about it with her. She told me that he was addicted to sex, only not with her.

That was when Debby started crying. I mean, really crying. Crying so hard she could not talk properly. I have never been good with crying women. I still remember hearing my mother cry so much when I was a little boy. Painful to hear. So I tried to talk to Debby. I tried to make her feel better so that she would stop her crying. I told her things would work out for the best. I said those things to her, Papa — even when I do not believe this for myself.

Tuesday 5th September 2000.
Karl Jnr won a merit award at school today — for excellent written composition. Maybe he takes after his mom, or after you, his GrandPapa Jerzy. Feel happy and proud!! So why can I not tell my son how proud I am of him? The words are always there, but they get caught in my throat, like fish bones. Why should it be so hard to praise someone you love? Feel scared. Because that is the sort of thing my father would have done. Piotr Pedanski never expressed anything but anger and disappointment. Must try to be a better father. Must. Must. Must!!

Friday 8th September 2000.
The monthly sales were held up in Chatfield today. I trucked up a dozen yearlings. Not my best stock, but they were the only ones I could choose. There must have been something out there again over the past few nights. The herd was very spooked. Jumping at the fences. A few had cut themselves up pretty bad. Cannot sell them

for a good price, not until they heal. So a dozen beasts was all I had.

The sale yards were half empty. Folks are still doing it tough after the dry weather and the fires. Not too many buyers either. I put my beasts out as two lots of six. I was hoping for forty-five hundred for the first lot and four thousand for the second. But the first lot sold for only two thousand and the second were passed in. I had not planned on having to truck beasts home again. No budget. So I sold them off to other ranchers — one by one. I made a measly twelve hundred dollars.

When it was finished, I went back to the truck and tried to work out how we could pay off nine thousand dollars' worth of debts with a little over three thousand. I decided at that point. There is no avoiding it now. Once he has healed completely, I am going to have to sell off Jerzy Six.

Oh Papa, how did you keep your head above water during all those dark years? How does a man survive the hard times?

Saturday 9th September 2000.
Spent the day mending fences where the yearlings had done damage. Tracks outside the fence too. Big paw prints. A big cat? No, even bigger. Feeling scared tonight, Papa. Very worried!!

Sunday 10th September 2000.
Sue did the laundry today and she found the sale
receipts for the yearlings in the pockets of my jeans.
She was real mad at me. I had told her I made enough
on the sales to break even with our debts. So I lied
to my wife. I told her I did not want her to worry.
Not completely true. What I really never want to be
is a failure. I do not want my wife to think of me
like that. I cannot stand the thought of her looking
at me with scorn — or worse — pity. But now I have
added lies to the mix of my sins. What a pathetic
man I am!!

Monday 11th September 2000.
Sue-Ellen went into Chatfield to see about part-time
work. Old man Darcy is always telling her he has a
position for her back at the drug store, if she ever wants
it. Tells everyone in town that Sue-Ellen McLean was
the best darn employee he ever had.

I told her not to do it. Darcy is a deviant. She once
told me he used to look up her skirt when she climbed
the store room ladder to reach high shelves. Now she
keeps telling me to relax. Darcy was way too old for
those things now. And just in case, she will wear jeans
if she gets a job back with him. We need the money. I
knew she was right. I still did not like it.

While Sue was in town, I drove out to Sandhills to see Debby. We had a nice time together. I told her about my money troubles and about Sue going back to work. I told her that I felt like a failure. Debby looked at me with her understanding eyes. Listened to me. Really listened. I truly believe she cares for me. It feels like I can tell her anything.

After I came home, I realized that I had not asked Debby about how she was going. I did not ask if she had been able to talk to Peter about those swing nights, and those things he was making her do. Papa, I am such a selfish person sometimes.

Tuesday 12th September 2000.

Got a letter in the mail today. IRS Audit notice. They have discovered some irregularities in my 1999 tax return. Therefore, two auditors will be visiting on Friday 22nd of this month. If this time is not suitable, I can make other arrangements.

An IRS audit. On top of everything else!! It felt like I would vomit when I read that letter. The stress. The stress!! I do not even remember where my return papers are for last year. I was too busy watching out for wild-fires and trying to survive. Must start looking. Perhaps they are in the cupboard under the stairs. I will go check now, before bed.

Wednesday 13th September 2000.
Sue-Ellen working today. Darcy gave her that old job back. She works on Wednesdays and Fridays. Extra shifts if she wants. I am not happy about it, but I did not say anything to Sue.

Found my shoe box of receipts for the IRS. They were up under the stairs. Now I must go and sort them out.

Thursday 14th September 2000.
Sue helped me sort out the IRS stuff today. Great girl. How fortunate am I to have such a wonderful wife!! Why am I not better at showing her how much she means to me? Feeling guilty and low. At least things are quiet out in the fields at the moment.

Saturday 16th September 2000.
Little Karl had an accident today. Took a tumble from the tire swing out back. Was trying to see how high he could make it go. Somehow he fell off and landed hard in the dirt. Busted up his right leg pretty good. Plenty of blood, but nothing seems broken. Mostly grazes from the rocks and dirt.

Sue-Ellen was real mad at me. Told me that swing has to go, before the boy kills himself. Do not want to do it. The boy loves playing on that swing. Maybe if he promises to be careful, his mom will change her mind. It is just another thing for me to worry about.

Monday 18th September 2000.
Karl Jnr tried to use his leg as an excuse not to go to school today. Sue furious!! The boy went to school and I spent the day up in the fields. Wise to keep clear of my wife when she is in these angry moods.

A nice day to be outdoors. Warm, especially for this time of year. You would like it here Papa, the Cottonwoods are beautiful, just starting to turn yellow and orange. The land is full of color. But dry. We need rain. Soon.

Wednesday 20th September 2000.
It is hard to believe we are almost in the fall. The first week of September was as hot as any I could remember. Daytimes still close to one hundred. It is still very dry. I had to un-bail some of my winter feed to keep the fat on my animals before the winter. That means we might have to buy feed if the winter is hard. Or sell more stock. But then…

I had got to thinking whatever had been attacking the animals had moved on. Nothing for weeks. I was starting to feel a little better about things. But it happened again last night. Something broke into the eastern field, killed two cows and half-ate one of them. In the far corner of the pasture, the dry ground was a riot of dust and blood and gore. The remaining beasts were huddled together on the house side of the field. I ran the fences, looking for clues as to what had attacked and where it or they had come in, but only found some blood scrapes on the lumber. The ground is too dry for tracks.

And then something happened. Even now, as I write these words Papa, I can see the image in my brain. I drove up to the northern end of Ranek Ranch, where the brush is closest to the fences. Boss and Aussie started howling in the tray of the truck. I followed their line of sight and saw something huge disappearing into the Juniper brush. I mean, really huge. Something dark and lumbering. I must be going crazy Papa, but I think it was a bear.

Grizzly…

Friday 22nd September 2000.
IRS Audit today. Two unsmiling auditors arrived wearing pinstripes and carrying ominous black brief cases. The man looked just like the sort of finance nerd the IRS would employ—sensible hair, pens in his shirt pocket and tinted lenses clipped onto his prescription glasses. He was so terrified of dogs, I had to lock Aussie and

Boss in the Blazer, then put the truck inside the barn, before he would even get out of his car.

His partner would have been very handsome — if she had been a man. She had a tanned angular face, hair tied back in a perfectly cylindrical ponytail, perfect white teeth and steely eyes like a toy action figure. It's been hours since they left, but I can still see those two faces perfectly. And yet, I do not remember either of their names.

The two of them stayed about five hours. I had been out all night. So tired. The audit was a blur. They kept shuffling papers and asking questions I could scarcely answer. I wished Sue had been there to help out, but she was working for Darcy today. I gave the auditors copies of everything they wanted. Went and let Boss and Aussie out of the truck just as they were leaving. Watched the guy running to his car. He ran like a scared little girl. Good to laugh!!

I do not know if our tax things are right now, or not. I cannot concentrate on all these things at the moment. It is happening to me again. Too much. Life is all too much.

Sunday 24th September 2000.
Spent Thursday and Friday night out in the Blazer. Two nights parked out in the field, fighting sleep and running a search light along the fence lines. I wanted to go out again last night, but Sue got upset. We had

an argument. Big one. Told me I had responsibilities to her and Karl Jnr. Told me one night would not make a difference. Even while I was arguing with her, I knew she was right. I was a mess. IRS Audits and ranch stuff. Everything getting on top of me. Plus, the weather has finally started to turn. The days will soon be busy. Stock need to be rounded up and penned down in the feed lots. Corralled. I need sleep.

I wanted to go see Debby yesterday, but she and Peter were away for the weekend up in South Dakota. Pastor stuff, or swinging, she would not say. Sue-Ellen tried to make love to me last night, but I was too tense. I could not ... I don't even want to write it down. A failure of the worst kind!! Sue did not say anything. She went and ran herself a bath. Her second for the evening. After a while I could hear rhythmic washing sounds. Whimpering. Pain or pleasure — I could not tell. Then she came back to bed. No words. Eventually I slept.

The nightmare struck again. More than one attacker this time — I am sure of it. I lost five cows, valuable stock, run down and torn apart. All five cows were pregnant. Yet not one of them was eaten. Whatever the hell was out there did not even have the decency to make a meal of my losses. No, to them I am nothing but sport. Now I know they are never going to stop. I have to do something about it. But what? How do you fight an enemy you don't really know? Can never see?

I cannot explain how hard it was to go back up to that field this morning. More gas. A lit match. Another funeral pyre. The rest of the day lost. I am losing. Papa help me, I am losing.

Monday 25th September 2000.
I cannot write tonight. I cannot think properly. Numb. Losing touch with reality. If reality ever existed. I want to run away again. Know I cannot. Help me Papa. Give me your words…

Tuesday 26th September 2000.
It is the waiting that is the worst. Waiting. Holding onto threads of hope — because things are seldom as bad as you fear. Waiting and worrying things will be worse. Why do I always worry myself into the middle of the worst possible thing? Why can I not feel positive anymore? Thank goodness I have these pages to write out my feelings, and my fingers have started to work again. I know that, without these words, I would surely go crazy.

Saturday 30th September 2000.
Spent more long nights running the fences. Shot a wild dog near the cows on Friday night. Must have been attracted by the smell of the blood or something. Big

dog, black with yellow eyes, like a wolf. When I hung his body off the willow tree, you could see he was over 5 feet long and maybe 75 pounds. Perhaps this is what is killing our beasts? Will have to keep going out. Dogs work in packs. There may be more of them. Is this it? No!! It cannot be. Not even a big pack of dogs would mess up a full-grown shorthorn bull like Jerzy Six. And what about that shape I saw in the Juniper a couple of weeks back?

Sunday 1st October 2000.

Word has been all over town for the last few days — and today it happened. Peter Clarke was on TV, leading a huge worship service up in Sioux. They made the program last week. That was why Debby was so secretive about last weekend. She could not say about the program until it was shown.

Peter looked magnificent, in his white robes and his powdery-pink face. He led the prayer part of the broadcast. He raised his hands towards heaven and he prayed for the lost; for the widows, for the sick, for those suffering under the 'burden of sin.' Then he said it... tears started rolling down his face, while he prayed for those who were locked in the 'devil's grip' of addiction. Alcohol or drugs or sexual perversion. He actually cried at this point. People in his congregation cried. They showed their faces on TV. People swept away by the godliness of this Pastor Clarke. I had to turn the TV off. So angry!!

Still tonight, hours later, I am so angry. Praying for the lost 'sinners', when he was doing those things himself. I wanted to call Debby to see if she was OK, but Sue-Ellen was around and I do not want her to know about what is happening with the Clarkes. I am so angry!! But I must try to sleep now.

Took the dog carcass down this afternoon. Sue has been real mad at me for hanging it on the willow tree. I think I will use it as bait. So much is happening. Must try to sleep.

Monday 2nd October 2000.
Took the dog carcass up on the back of the dirt bike and set it down about twenty yards from the stud bulls — about halfway to the brush. Sat out in the cold for hours. Nothing.

Tuesday 3rd October 2000.
Sat out again tonight. Took the truck this time, so I wouldn't be so cold. Crows had been making hell with the carcass during the day. A couple of foxes came in right on dusk. A Coyote after it got really dark. Did not bother shooting. We cannot afford to waste ammunition.

Will need to get more soon. Some .375 rounds for the Winchester and maybe a few clips for my AR15. I will write a note to remind myself.

Wednesday 4th October 2000.
Black today. Achieved nothing. Wasted day. Wasted. Wasted!!

Friday 6th October 2000.
Black day. Black. Black. Black. Black. Black. Black. Black. Black!!
    Papa, help me!!

Sunday 8th October 2000.
Another very black day today. Burning. Drowning in the flames. Sue and I have been arguing a lot. We had another big one tonight. And even as I write this I could not tell you why. Too many things. We argued about everything and nothing. Have to try better. Have to be a better husband. My wife deserves that. Made too many mistakes in the past. I am not going to do that to my Sue.

    Ranchers' Association meeting in town tomorrow. Not sure if I am looking forward to that or not. Maybe someone else is going through these attacks? Cannot imagine it is just confined to our ranch. Perhaps they will have a plan. Tomorrow may be a brighter day.

Monday 9th October 2000.

A dirty low day today. The fall meeting of the Panhandle Ranchers' Association. They held the meeting in the hall at St Patrick's Church in Chatfield. But there was nothing godly about what took place in that hall. Nothing at all. Do you know how the swing and sway of laughter can bury a man? Burn his soul. I was buried today. Buried and burned. And I was not even dead. I plan to resign from that Association — first chance I get.

I waited until the end of the meeting to say my piece. Figured someone else in the region was having the same problems I was. They had to be. But when it came to the last orders of business, and since no one had spoke up, I figured it was my time. So I raised my hand and told them what had been happening. Told them everything I could remember. Told them what I thought it was.

Bear? Chip Fontana had bellowed. Chip was the Association Vice-President; a dark rolling thunderstorm of a man. A Grizzly!! Where you think you are boy? Goddamn Yellowstone?

Others began to join in.

No bears been in this State for 100 years, and they were Blacks.

Black bear ain't gonna tackle a full-grown Shorthorn, Karl.

Come on boy — next you is gonna tell us you gotta circle the wagons at night to keep the Sioux at bay.

That last one was Marlon Walker, oldest rancher in the Association. And that was it. Once he spoke up, well that was when they all started chipping in.

Maybe you need a vacation.

Or more sleep.

You been spending too many nights pleasuring that pretty young wife of yours.

Man can have too much of a good thing.

The laughs started swinging across that hall. Laughter echoing on the timber floor. Rolling like waves. Crashing over me. I started to get to my feet. A man can only take so much humiliation.

Finally, as I made to leave, the President spoke. Art Clayton is a third generation cattle rancher. Irish Catholic. A hard man. Unblinking stone face that belonged up on Mount Rushmore. Hard man, yes, but he was just as well.

He asked me if I had considered a Mountain Lion. Said it just as I was making to leave. Told me there were plenty of them in the hills around my land.

And the meeting fell in around their all-knowing President.

46

That might be what you have.

Of course—a Cougar.

Set yourself some traps.

Take your dogs out. Pack a decent shooter. Problem will be licked in days.

And just like that, they had me sorted out. Only I knew they did not. I have seen what a Cougar does to a deer. This is different. I know it. Not dogs and not a big cat.

I went straight from the meeting to Seymour's, and spent the last of my cash on ammo.

Peter Clarke was on a pastors' retreat in Kansas City for a week, so after I left the Chatfield town limits, I took a sixty mile detour and went home via Debby's place. I needed to see her. Unload. But when I got out there, all I could do was collapse into her lap and wail like a child.

I am losing it again, Papa. Hang on. I must hang on!!

Tuesday 10th October 2000.

Could not move today. Stayed in the house. Silent. What if they are right and I am a failure? I am a failure. I am a failure. I am a failure. I am a failure. I am a failure. I am a failure. I am a failure. I am a failure. I am a failure. Yes Papa, I am!!

Wednesday 11th October 2000.

Sue-Ellen left early for Darcy's this morning. The old guy was going out of town today and she was going to be responsible for the whole store. Peter Clarke was still in Kansas on his Pastor's retreat. There was only one place I was heading today.

It felt so good to be in Debby's arms, but right away I knew something was wrong. We went inside and she made coffee. We made small talk. The second Presidential debate was on tonight—Bush and Gore. Neither of us thought we would bother watching. When the coffees were made, we went into the lounge room and sat in the semi-dark. We sat silent, listening to their old grandfather clock ticking and tocking and ticking and tocking...

When I asked her if something was wrong, all she would say was she could not go on this way. Cried. I did not say anything. Did not have the right words. I was wondering how I could keep going myself. It seems that neither of us have the answers.

But Debby could not stay quiet. She told me about her last weekend. She and Peter had gone over to Cheyenne for a swing date. Only this time, there was only one other person involved—another man. And Peter had sat back in that man's recliner, smoked one of that man's fat Cuban cigars, and watched that man have sex with his wife.

I sat and listened to her, my fists clenching so tight they began to ache. Felt so very cold.

Papa, it was awful!!

Debby has told me before how she copes with these nights. How she goes numb to it all and pretends she is in a movie or a play. How sometimes she even manages to enjoy herself—only to feel guilty afterwards. But this time…well this time was just the end for her.

I told her she should leave her husband. The whole President Clinton scandal had showed American women they could stand up and be strong—even when dealing with the most powerful men.

She shook her head. Told me I did not understand. Peter had friends everywhere. He was beyond reproach. His untarnished reputation would destroy her. She would be made to look like the sinner. Where would she go? Back to her people near Austin? Hog farming? No. She told me she had made vows to God. She promised to love her husband for better and for worse. She said she was going to keep trying.

Then Debby asked me how I was going since Monday. How things had gone at the Ranchers' meeting. I had wanted to tell her about my humiliation—about how low they had made me feel—but after hearing her story, I did not think I could share something so trivial.

So there we were. Two people stuck. Buried in holes, not of our own making. Buried in holes too deep. I cannot see the light above me anymore, Papa. How do I climb out?

Friday 13th October 2000.
Sue-Ellen has been very excited tonight. Darcy just had his best month in ten years. The store had been losing customers to the new twenty-four hour discount drug store across town, but things are turning around. Darcy told Sue it was because of her. The customers love her. Darcy loves her. Everyone loves her. I wish I knew how to love her better. Had a beer tonight for my wife. Cheers to Sue-Ellen. I wish I had more beers. Need to feel happy. But I cannot stop thinking about poor Debby and what she is going through.

Sunday 15th October 2000.
There is a color the sun goes, right on sunset, when it peeks out from beneath the heavy grey clouds. It is a special kind of sunset color—not orange and not gold—something else. I was working in the main barn and I noticed everything outside had turned the color of copper. So I went out, sat on a corner fence post and watched that sun sink into the hills.

And at one point it was like looking at the whole world from inside a glass of whiskey. Made me wish I could afford a bottle or two. Drank my last beer yesterday. No spare cash for booze. Need to feel numb. I'm losing it again.

Monday 16th October 2000.
Started digging drainage around the winter feedlots. Worked hard. Maybe two hundred yards done. The earth like concrete. Tired tonight. Been good to work away some of the stress. I need sleep.

Friday 20th October 2000.
Digging drainage all week. My joints feel like they are welding together. Hard to move. Anyway, the western feedlot is finished, but that was the easy one. Eastern feedlot is usually the wet one. It needs hundreds of yards work.

Sue-Ellen got a pay rise today. Bless her heart. Will help pay off a few of the tabs I have run up in town. But I feel guilty about it. I am the man of the family. Surely it is my responsibility to pay for the well-being of my family. Or am I too old-fashioned? After all, mother raised her children almost on her own. I would be proud to be half as good a provider as she was. And you, Papa. If only I could.

Monday 23rd October 2000.

Spent the day sitting on my ass in the middle of a drainage ditch. Winter is finally in the air. So much work to be done, but I sat in the ditch and watched the afternoon turn the sky all burning pink and gold. And I watched ten thousand snow geese flying south. They flew in dark wedges that cut against that screaming sky, flying from horizon to horizon. I wondered if they were flying somewhere better?

Tuesday 24th October 2000.

I am full of foreboding tonight, Papa, and I do not know why.

Thursday 26th October 2000.

Numb tonight. My mouth will not work. My heart feels like it is scarcely beating. I could not eat a bite of dinner.

Art Clayton called by the house about four. I had just come back in from the eastern feedlot, my clothes covered in dirt and my body full of aches. Art told me Dan Rensburg had died. One of his ranch hands found him down by Chatfield Creek. He was sitting in the front seat of his brand new Toyota pickup. The engine still running. A hose ran from the tail pipe into the cab.

I have never written about Dan before, Papa. His

ranch is about two miles to the east of here. The two of us never really spoke much. Not that we had any problems with each other, he was just a quiet sort of guy. Did his own thing. Ran Angus cattle and the new Wagyu breed that the Japanese folks like. He was the first member of the Association to try that breed. At the last association meeting he told us he could get almost twice the price per pound exporting his meat to Japan. The Japanese like marbled beef, and they are eating more and more of it each year. Dan knew how to seize an opportunity.

Dan had a wife and three beautiful little girls. He had everything to live for. Give me strength — he was only thirty five years old.

What if that was me? Papa, what if that was me? I know it could have been me.

Friday 27ᵗʰ October 2000.

Worked hard on the drainage today. Did not want to give myself time to think. Dan Rensburg was a good rancher. Making money. Always trying new ideas. So why? Why him? His funeral is on Monday. They are burying him with his people over in Iowa.

Must stop thinking!! I need a drink tonight. The house is dry. Must stop writing. It causes me to think. Thinking feels dangerous tonight.

Saturday 28th October 2000.

Noticed the first snow of the fall was on the hills this morning, gleaming white among the gold and grey brush. Pretty. Finished running new drainage around the eastern feedlot. Should be less of a mud heap this winter. Back real painful.

Monday 30th October 2000.

Spent the morning on my dirt bike, herding with Boss and Aussie. Riding around on autopilot. Started with the breeding cows, but I had to stop when the bike broke down. Could not get it to start again. Pushed the thing back to the barn with Aussie sitting on the back and Boss trailing faithfully behind.

Horsed around with the bike and managed to get it started again, but noticed that Aussie had a limp. He was lifting his right front paw. So left him back at the house and finished bringing the cows in with good old Boss. Boss would keep working even if all four legs were crippled. He is the best dog a man could own.

Noisy night tonight. Sue-Ellen and Karl Jnr are in bed, but with so many beasts in the feedlots close to the house, there is always something making a sound. I'm out on the porch with Boss, sitting under the light and writing to the bellow of agitated shorthorns. At least they are close to home now. Should be safe.

There is a bright star out east tonight, Papa. In the sky over Iowa. They would have buried Dan in Oskaloosa today. I hope he can rest in peace now. I hope we all can.

Tuesday 31ˢᵗ October 2000.
Aussie still limping this morning, but seems a little better. Happy about that. No money for vet bills right now. And Little Karl is upset about his pet. Refused to go to school. Did not even want to go trick-or-treating this evening. We had another family argument.

There is always something!!

Wednesday 1ˢᵗ November 2000.
Aussie OK today, but it was too wet to do any herding. Gave both dogs a rest. Rang Debby after Sue-Ellen went to work. It is the first time we have talked for a while.

Debby seems better. She told me that Peter had agreed to go and see a therapist with her, providing it was in another state, where he wasn't so well known. She has found one in Denver and even though it is a 600 mile round trip, they are going to give it a try. They are going to have a weekend away for just the two of them.

I am glad she sounded happier. Perhaps there is hope. Perhaps.

Thursday 2nd November 2000.

Wet again. No herding. At one point I sat in the kitchen and stared out the window and I watched the rain falling across the fields. I noticed the last of the leaves on the willow tree. They were all orange and shiny from the rain. Papa, I remember how you once told me that the rain makes everything new. You showed me how the leaves on the trees would glisten and glow, and the air would smell fresh and alive again. Perhaps, after all of this rain has finished, things will be fresh and alive again on my ranch.

Sunday 5th November 2000.

Wet all weekend. Sue-Ellen went to church in Chatfield. Boss and I watched TV. Bored, but not as depressed as I expected. I hope that is a sign of things to come. The promise of a fresh start.

Monday 6th November 2000

First time we have seen the sun in days. Happy with the work I did in the eastern feedlot. A lot less muck and mud than last year. Lost a few beasts due to that sludge in the past. Cannot afford that this year. Sat on the porch with Boss and the newspaper and I enjoyed a little sunshine.

In this morning's edition of the Journal I found a small article—almost missed it, with all the election nonsense around—two teenage boys had been camping up on the Reservoir, not five miles from Ranek Ranch. These kids claimed they saw a brown bear in the brush near their campsite. The Park service investigated and found no trace of bears of any kind. A case of mistaken identity. Perhaps the boys had been drinking or taking drugs.

Or perhaps…

Tuesday 7th November 2000.

Quiet day on the ranch. Busy day for America. Election day. Sue-Ellen went and voted in Chatfield. Her family has always voted Republican. Many Nebraskans do. I do not vote. Papa, American politics confuses me. It is more like a TV show, with big stars and rock bands and colored balloons. No, people craving power should never be trusted with it. All evening, every TV station, every radio broadcast is about the damned election. Even now, late in the night as I am writing, no one seems to know who has won. The Democrats have won more votes, but the Republicans seem to have more States. Except no one agrees who has won Florida. The whole leadership of this country might be decided by a few votes in Florida. Sometimes I wonder Papa—is this kind of democracy such a good thing? Still, it is nice to have something to think about, other than the ranch.

Wednesday 8th November 2000.

Ground dry enough to get back out on the bike today. Good day of herding. Aussie showing no ill-effects from his leg injury and he worked like a little star. Boss worked himself to exhaustion again. Dogs are just great. They give so much and expect so little. I wish people were the same.

Monday 13th November 2000.

Have spent the week sorting out beasts into feedlots and worming. My arms are raw from rubbing on fences and being drooled on by beasts as they got the drench gun. Still, as I write to you tonight, I feel like the worst might be behind us.

Most of the cattle are now close to the house, in feed-lots or barns. They should be safe from being attacked now. I think we are better prepared for the winter than before, as long as the feed holds out. The drainage is much better. My work might be making a difference. This is a good feeling. Sue-Ellen told me I should feel satisfied with what I have achieved. Perhaps she is right.

And I have had two offers to buy Jerzy Six at the last sale before Christmas. Good offers. He is almost good again. A couple of weeks in a corral, putting on some extra pounds, and we will be looking good. We might even get more than we expect. Pay some debts. Move forward into the spring.

I hope, Papa. I hope so much!!

Tuesday 14th November 2000.

Been chased by a feeling all day. Cannot shake it. Something bad is coming. The feeling prowls through my head, clawing at my temples. I close my eyes, tight, try to make it go away, but it will not. Something bad is coming. And I do not know if I will be able to handle it.

Wednesday 15th November 2000.

Big storm running tonight. We lost the electricity just after supper. Sue-Ellen and Little Karl have gone to bed. I have been doing things by lantern. Brought the dogs inside. Let them sleep in the kitchen — even if it gets me yelled at by Sue in the morning. But we might get snow. And the dogs are important to helping me bring the two big bulls in. Will do that tomorrow, if the weather is OK.

I am listening to the battery radio. Waiting for the weather forecast, but getting endless reports about the election results. Everyone seems to think Bush will win the White House, but the result is going to court. Finally the weather came on. It sounds like we might have a break tomorrow. I should go to bed. Want to get those two big boys into their barn before a really big snow dump.

Thursday 16th November 2000.

Though there had been snow up on the hills since the end of October, today was the first time we have seen flakes on Ranek Ranch. It started last night and though it did not lay on the ground, the air is silver and heavy with ice. Most of the cattle have been corralled now, there was just a straggler or two and the two stud bulls out on the fences. Except, now it is one.

This morning I found Jerzy Two down near the house barn. He had broken through the fences of his own field. I thought it must have been the storm, but he was unusually upset and aggressive. It took me over an hour to get him into the barn, into a pen and settled. I feared the worst for his big friend.

Jerzy Six had been recovering well from the wounds he'd suffered back at the end of summer. But when I found him today, he was in a terrible state. Gouged and bitten. A huge flap of skin and flesh swinging from his left flanks. A front leg busted. Ordinarily I would have put him to the bullet, but he was a valuable animal. Worth thousands. I had at least two good offers for him. I had to give him every chance. For me too…

After all the bad weather, the vet at Chatfield was busy, so he phoned his associate to come up from Red Springs. She was a short girl, Hispanic, perhaps forty years old, kind of pretty. She followed me up to the top field in her little Toyota RV. Stepped out of her car and immediately shook her head.

Cougar? I asked her.

Not like any Mountain Lion I've ever seen, she told me. A pride of lions in Africa maybe. She paused for a second, her hand on her chin. Then she said, you know, last time I saw a big animal as messed up as this was an old man moose, back when I was working for the Parks Service up in Yeller. But that was a Grizzly.

We stood in silence for a few moments. Jerzy Six staggered and fell. Gave an awful, heart-rending bellow. And I knew he was not going to be able to get himself up again. The vet and I looked at each other. We both knew at that point.

She asked me if I wanted her to do it. But I could hear in her voice that she did not want to.

No, I told her, it is my responsibility.

I put Jerzy Six down as soon as she left. Gave him two from the Winchester, just to make sure he did not suffer. Then I sat in the cabin of my truck and wept and wept.

And I never did find out what that vet's name was. I wish I had asked, Papa. It seems very important to me now. Perhaps she could have rung Chip Fontana or Marlon Walker and told them what she had seen. But it will not happen. It is all down to me.

I cannot believe we have gone backwards again. It is not fair, Papa. It is just not fair at all.

Friday 17th November 2000.
The Bank Manager called today. Can you believe the timing? After the hell I was going through. He called about our missed payments. Our loans are all in arrears. He wanted to come out and discuss the issues. Assess our situation. He wanted to sort it out before Thanksgiving. I had no intention of telling him about our lost stock. Or how my biggest asset was now lying out there in the mud, rotting. So I told him to go to hell. Hung up in his ear.

I just know he will call back. And I do not think I can handle it.

Saturday 18th November 2000.
I can't handle it. I can't handle it. I can't handle it.

Sunday 19th November 2000.
Black today. Hot and frozen. Feel like I am being crushed from within. Pressure. I have to hang on. Nights in the darkness. Days even worse. Death is everywhere I look.

Monday 20th November 2000.
Debby called me tonight, while I was sitting in my truck, up in the top field. The therapy session in Denver went

very well. Peter has agreed to go to a rehab center in Connecticut for people with addiction issues. He has cancelled two planned swing dates. Trashed all the porn he had hidden away. I could hear the relief in her voice.

Papa, I am trying to feel happy for Debby, even after another fruitless evening out in the field. Even though my world is crumbling. Perhaps tomorrow will be better. I need to keep believing this!!

Tuesday 21st November 2000.

I have been sitting with Jerzy Six's carcass for the past five nights. Camped out in the Blazer with Boss, and my Winchester. Waiting for the hunter—or hunters—to come and claim their prize. Five long, cold nights, trying not to think too much about anything. Trying not to wilt under the pressure.

Every once in a while Boss would snarl or bark me awake. I would switch on the spotlight on the roof of the truck and surprise some animal roaming the edge of the brush just outside my fences: a couple of foxes, a Coyote, but mostly just rabbits. Snow swirling and dazzling the eyes.

It is two days to Thanksgiving. Sue was mad as hell with me for going out so much. She wants us to have a quiet, pleasant holiday together. I cannot see how that is possible.

Wednesday 22nd November 2000.

I should have gone out again last night. I had a nightmare instead. I was visited by a dead man. Dan Rensburg came to see me. I could see his face, just like he was still alive. He got me out of bed and took me out to the back porch. Then, as we sat under the naked willow tree, under Little Karl's tire swing, he told me everything was OK. Things weren't so bad on the other side. He actually told me that. He told me it would be OK to come across, if I ever felt like doing it. I woke up soaking wet and shivering. Is he right Papa? Are things OK on the other side? I am terrified to go back to sleep!!

It was a cold clear day today. I brought the last few stragglers down into the feedlots. Then I drove out to Sandhills, after Sue went into town to work. Peter Clarke was out visiting the flock for Thanksgiving, drinking a million cups of coffee and getting fatter on pastries and pumpkin pie. Debby seemed surprised to see me. Told me Peter could come home at any time. She did not want anything upsetting him, not while things were so delicately balanced. I did not care. I told her I needed her.

So Debby took me to their lounge room, we sat down, and I collapsed into her chest. Sobbing. She stroked my hair as I rocked back and forth in the warm sanctuary of her breasts. My body gasping. Bawling. I could not stop it. Why is my life not improving? When will it be my turn to cross over to the other side? Something bad is coming for me.

I do not want to sleep tonight. I am afraid.

Thursday 23ʳᵈ November 2000.

Thanksgiving. The arguments started around midday. Sue did not want me going out. Told me the animals were now all safe in their corrals or in feedlots close to the house. No need to go out waiting for something that might never come back. We had had some tough times, but we still had each other and it was proper that we spend time together as a family on Thanksgiving. I knew she was right Papa, but that did not stop me yelling back at her.

By afternoon things were real ugly. Sue had forgotten to put the turkey into the oven on time. Blamed me. And the bird sat on the kitchen counter, raw and naked, while the two of us screamed and hollered and dragged up all the things we hated about each other. That was when I saw our son.

Karl Jnr had taken himself outside. There he was, sitting in the gloom, swaying slowly on the tire swing. He was staring out across the pink and silver of last light. Outside, where it was beautiful. Trying to ignore the ugly world his parents had created inside.

He had his hands over his ears.

That did it. That was enough.

It had been expected — the total blackness — but I could not stop it. I staggered out to the back porch. Then, in the glow of the porch light, I stood like a broken man and wondered why I felt so terrified. Breaths blowing in and out of my dusty mouth. Time was racing. Days, weeks, years were lost. I yelled at Karl Jnr to go back inside with his mother. Then I collapsed on the porch, clutching for my knees and drawing them to my chest. I began rocking back and forth, silently begging the darkness to leave me in peace. I was alone. I could not go to see Debby. I could not bring myself to confide in my wife, or my son. Even Dan Rensburg had left me. So alone.

And then, when freedom seemed to be impossible, something told me what I had to do. I heard your words Papa. You told me I had to get out of that house. I had to solve this thing. Tonight was going to be the night. Tonight I was going to fight back. Thanksgiving be damned.

I loaded Boss into the Blazer, while Sue screamed hell at me from the back porch. I took my ArmaLite with me this time. My AR15, with the modified firing mechanism and two full clips of NATO ammo. No jerking around. Whatever was out there, I was going to find it and shoot it to hamburger. Then I was going to shovel the whole bloody mess into the back of my pick-up and pour it out on Chip Fontana's front lawn. Then, maybe he and his buddies could take a vacation from being smart-asses.

The night was colorless and unsteady. The snow began coming down harder as I drove further from the house, swinging across my headlights from right to left, settling like melted plastic on the truck windshield before the wipers swept it away. Boss began whimpering as we bounced over the tire tracks towards the field where Jerzy Six still lay rotting. I did not know what he knew. I did not know what was out there. What had taken the huge beasts' life, but then I saw something in the swirling snow flurries…

…four pinpricks of light. Swinging and swaying in the darkness. Two pairs of glowing, burning eyes, close together, buried in grey mountains of flesh and fur. Rising and falling. Swinging and swaying.

Grizzlies.

Papa, we live in Nebraska. The nearest bears are more than four hundred miles away, up in Yellowstone. How the hell was it possible? But when I looked again, there they were. No mistake. No mistake!!

I switched off the truck, my hand reaching across the back of the seat to where my rifle was lying. Hands shaking. Heart beating now. Really beating. Excited or terrified? Both.

I remember thinking out loud—gently now, calm heart, steady.

Boss was going berserk on the seat beside me. Roaring barks, his claws digging and scratching at the passenger side window. The two bears held their ground. With the moonlight and snow, I could just make out the silhouettes of their bodies. Hunched backs. Two males. Big. Papa, they were so big!! I held the ArmaLite close, marveling as the cold metal warmed with the blood. Man and machine as one. I sat and watched. Waiting for the two huge beasts to settle back on the carcass. Then it would be time...

I took the safety off my rifle, switched it to automatic and, gently, I unlatched the door of the Blazer. Then I hit the spot beams up on the roof and went out fast. Boss went out too, before I could stop him. I can still remember the scene. It is vivid in my mind. The two bears rose up on their hind legs, twisting and falling into retreat. Boss was almost onto them, barking and snarling like a mad dog. I could not get in a shot, not without risking hitting my buddy. The two huge beasts effortlessly slipped through the lumber of my fences and Boss leapt after them. In seconds, all three were lost in the brush.

I heard roars and yelping. I went through the fence and into the brush. Darkness. Branches cracking in front of me. It sounded like hell. The noise. The noise!! I couldn't see anything. Had to back away. Too dangerous.

I went back to the truck and waited for Boss to come back. I waited for maybe an hour. The snow began to fall heavier. There was no sign. My buddy. My Boss. I can't believe it. What have I done to you?

Friday 24th November 2000.

It was just after midnight when I came back to the house. Thanksgiving was over and Sue-Ellen was gone. She left me a plate of roast turkey and mashed potatoes — both now cold — and a slice of pumpkin pie. She had left a note on the kitchen counter. She had taken Little Karl and they were going to spend time with her folks. She wrote me she did not know when she would be back, but when she was, we were going to talk about selling the ranch.

I switched off the kitchen lights and just sat there. Failed again. Failed. Perhaps my father had been right about me. Too much of a dreamer. Too soft. Too much like you, Papa Jerzy. Father once told me you were born to fail!!

I went back out at first light this morning. Thought about taking Aussie, to help me track the bears, but

I did not want to lose another dog, and besides, we gave Aussie to Little Karl when he was just a pup. The boy loves that dog. So I went on my own. Took the ArmaLite and all the clips I had. Parked the truck next to the spot where the two bears went through the fence, and I went after them on foot.

Despite the overnight snow, it was not hard to find their trail. The three of them left a wide path of beat up brush and busted branches. A hundred yards into the woods, I found my poor Boss. He was a mess. They had torn him up pretty bad, but not eaten him. They broke him like he was just a toy. His busted body was frozen in the snow.

I brought Boss back to the house and buried him under the willow out back. The tree with the tire swing. I tried to pray some words for him Papa, but nothing came out. So I thanked him for being so brave, and for trying to save my sorry hide when I had done nothing to deserve it.

When it was over, I went inside, washed the dirt off my hands, and rang the Clarke's number. Debby had told me not to call anymore. Peter was becoming suspicious. Folks told him they had seen my Blazer parked up at his house while he was away. A few times. After Clinton and Lewinski, it seems everyone in America thinks their loved ones are having affairs. But how could Rev

Clarke be a suspicious man? Considering what he used to do for a hobby!! Why would a man like that have any cause for suspicion or jealousy? Besides, nothing had happened between me and his wife. Nothing like that. So I tried to call her — and to hell with her deviant husband. But she was not there. The line rang out.

So now I am here, with my pen and journal, trying to hang on. Trying to hang on to you. Hang on to anything. Hard to see. Lights flashing in a dark room. Cannot swallow. Pain. Pain. Pain!! Why is this happening to me, Papa? What have I done to deserve this?

I was born to fail. It is clear to me now. Born to fail. Born to fail. Born to fail. Born to fail. Born to fail. Born to fail. Born to fail. Born to fail, just like you.

Hang on. Hang on. Hang on. Hang on!!

But I cannot hang on. Not like this.

It is time. Yes!!

Dan was right.

The time is now.

Hold on Boss. Hold on for just a little longer old buddy. Papa, prepare a place for your Karol. I am coming...

PART 3 — THE SWING

The writing trails off at this point. A few aimless scribbles in blue ink. A tear out of one corner of the page. I close his journal and lay it on my lap. The top book in the pile. The last he'd used. His last words and thoughts. I promised myself I wouldn't cry. Don't.

So, when had he written all these things? At night while I slept? While I was away in town? And had I missed that much of his life? The damn terrible things he'd seen up in our fields. What he'd faced. How he'd sheltered me from all that terribleness. And why hadn't I picked up on the thing he was having with Debby Clarke? Did I really believe him when he wrote it was nothing sexual?

Yes.

But why hadn't folks picked up on Peter Clarke, after all those years? In a county like this? The Clarkes left the State a few years back. A happy retirement in Florida. No one was any the wiser. I guess even small towns can still keep secrets. But my Karl knew. He held so many secrets. And he wrote such beautiful words in those pages. They were haunting words too.

Gosh, he'd written all this over ten damn years ago. Twelve. You hear people say it, and it sounds dumb, but I honestly don't know where those years went. It's only when I look in the mirror—and I see the first silver hairs winding across my head, or the crow's feet scratching at the corners of my eyes—that I realize I'm not in my twenties any more. Some days I feel a lot older than forty two.

Out through the cobwebs and dusty glass I see the old willow tree. Threadbare. Arthritic. The left hand branches torn away in the storms a few years ago. And that swing. You can imagine how much I want to tear that damn thing down. But I can't. I can't come within ten feet of that tree. Not now. And maybe never.

Another day has almost gone. Days move faster now. Seasons. Years. Folks say you have to move on, but I can't. I've tried. I can't. I put his journal down on the coffee table. Get up. Put on a CD. Don't even check the cover. I hit the random button and the Stones start playing. *No Expectations*. I hear the wavering cry of a slide guitar—Brian Jones—now deceased. The haunting, almost icy piano notes—Nicky

Hopkins — now deceased. A favorite song of Karol
Pedanski — now deceased.

I close my eyes to listen to the music, and it's Sunday
the twenty sixth of November, 2000. Again. The scene
is cut into my eyes. Damn it, I can't make it go away.

From the front gate of Ranek Ranch, you can see
the farm house, some of the barns, and the willow tree
with the swing tied to it. It was late on that Sunday
afternoon — maybe four or five — and the light was
getting low. Little Karl was asleep on the back seat, so
I got out and opened the gate myself — it was usually
the boy's job.

I noticed it after I got back in the car. The silhouette
of that old tree had changed. Something was hanging off the branch diagonally opposite the tire swing.
Something long and dark. Karl had sometimes hung
dogs or Coyotes off that branch, when he'd shot one
for harassing the calves. It used to drive me crazy, but
he still did it. Except November wasn't calving time.
And whatever was swinging off that branch was too
big to be a Coyote.

When I got closer I saw it.

I saw him.

Oh Karl. Karl…

I had the peace of mind to park out front, instead of
the back barn, where my little Honda usually lived. I

hustled little Karl inside, told him to go run himself a tub before dinner. Drew the drapes across all the back windows. Called 911.

After they'd pulled his body down, and after they asked me to identify him as my husband, the police found a shallow underneath the old willow tree. It was dug up as part of the investigation. I'd not even noticed one of the dogs was missing when I first came home. Dogs were the least of my concerns that day. Boss was like Karl's shadow. A big loyal moose of a dog. Strong as a bull. I still remember what the deputy told me when he came inside…

'I ain't never heard of no man bein' able to do that to no dog. Not shot. Not stabbed. No, there's somethin' funny goin' on here ma'am.'

The Park Service trapped two Grizzlies in the winter of 2001, after a tourist was mauled on a hiking trail in the Chatfield State Forest. Made news all across the country. No Grizzly Bears had been seen in Nebraska for maybe one hundred and fifty years. They were two big males. Possibly brothers. Authorities said they'd probably come down from Yellowstone, driven away by a lack of food and territory. Told locals to be wary, because more might be around. I remember being scared at night, in case there were any more around. I had no idea we'd already been visited by them — how much they had already impacted our lives — not until I read Karl's journals. It all could have been stopped. If only folks had listened to him.

This bed feels emptier tonight. Emptier than ever. I've slept by myself since 2000, but tonight the sheets feel cold and alone. He revisited me in those pages. I caught a glimpse of him again. As I read, I could hear him talking. The fear in his voice. The terrible blackness.

I'm not going to cry!

You have no idea how angry I've been with him — in the past and again tonight. Why couldn't he have just talked to me? I was his damn wife, there's nothing he could have told me that I wouldn't have tried to help him with. Maybe I could have helped him stay alive. I wish I had answers. I wish he was still here with me.

They held the funeral for him at St Pat's. Not a big turnout. Karl never made many friends. I think some came out of obligation. Little Karl and I sat down the front. He was so brave, my little guy. He read the eulogy to his dad. He never cried once.

A few of Karl's ranch buddies came. Sat down at the back of the church with my folks. And when it was over, they all stood around like park monuments. Nothing to say. What did you say to the grieved widow of another mid-west train wreck? Certainly, no one used the word 'suicide', but I really wished they had. And I wished those boys'd learnt how to talk about what was ailing them. Worrying them. Perhaps it might have saved good men like Dan Rensburg and Karl Pedanski — and those that have followed. The statistics are still a damn disgrace. So many men, with so much to live for. A wound to the heartland. America's unspoken shame.

I must have slept. Morning comes as a real surprise. Sun like a spotlight in my face. And the phone ringing.

'Hello?'

'Mom … Karl.'

'Morning darling, how's Kansas this morning?' I yawn and stretch.

'Oh, same old same old. Made my numbers last month, so Chuck has been off my back for a change.'

'Mmmmm … that's my boy.'

'Yeah.'

Silence on the line. I knew what he was going to ask me next.

'So, you going OK?'

'Yeah, I'm good sweetheart.'

'Been a long time coming.'

'Yeah, it has.'

'But I'm glad mom. I worry about you out there all on your own. You held onto that place for too long…'

I don't reply. We both know why…

'So you and Grandma Mabel huh?'

'Yep.'

'Should be interesting.'

'She'll be fine. She mellowed a lot since your Grandpa John died.'

'But why stay up there? Shoulda come out this way.'

'Never catch me dead in Tornado Alley. You know that.'

'Yeah, I know. Perhaps I should come over soon … get my haircut at Giovanni's … might as well keep the old family tradition alive while he's still there.'

'Giovanni always cut your hair so cute.'

'Yeah, that's not the look I'm after mom. Anyway, what time the movers coming?'

'Ten, I think.'

'Then you goin' straight up?'

'Everything is gone, no sense hanging around.'

Hanging around. Hanging around. Stupid! And that's when I start thinking about it again. That tire swing. That damn old rag-head of a willow tree. My Karl…

'Mom? Mom? You still there?'

'Yeah, sorry baby. Look, I've got a few things to do. Thanks for calling. I'll call you from Gran's place, so you know I got there safe.'

'Oh, OK … bye.'

I put down the phone and walk out to the back porch. Karl's big old splitter is still leaning against the corner of the house, near the chopping block, where he'd last used it. I pick it up. Heavy. The head is dark brown, dotted with spots of bright orange rust. The handle chocolate-brown and oily smooth. I pick up the splitter and start walking towards that ugly green and silver willow tree. I walk right underneath it, to the branch where the tire swing still hangs on threadbare lengths of yellow rope. The tire is cracked and grey, like the flesh of a corpse. Cobwebs inside the casing. A hateful thing.

I pick up that splitter, and with everything I have in my body, I take a swing…

'LOSING THE
POSTER'

AUSTIN TX

DAN 4 DANICA

DAN RENSBURG CLOSES HIS MATH BOOK, AND HE KINDA sighs. Got a headache, because math is hard. Harder'n hell. Real hard. Dan ain't too good at math, but then he ain't too good at any school stuff. "Dummy Dan", that's what they used to call him in elementary school. Now he were in junior high they just called him DD.

Dan hates that junk, but knows he can't do nothin' about it. Oh man, he wishes he were smart like his brother and sister. Dunstan was a Lieutenant in the Army. He'd been to Iraq. Were goin' to Afghanistan next. Fightin' them Telly-ban. Dan would often think about all them soldiers under his leading. Doin' what he told them to do. Yeah, Dunstan sure was smart. So was Janet. She were at college in Chicago. The Illinois University. Learning herself to be a animal doctor. Dan ain't like them at all. Things went kinda wrong in his brain. Or maybe every family has to have a dummy.

Dan's folks keep tellin' him it's OK. He don't have to be the same as them others. He just has to try to do his best. That's what his folks keep tellin' him. And if he does his best, then his dad has made him a promise. If those grades improve, the two of them are gonna take the best vacation ever! Because Austin is the only place for a guy to be in November.

Dan looks at the front cover of his math book. His stickers and his pictures and the junk he has wrote. It's all about her. Her teams. Her sponsors. Pictures of her and her cars. At the bottom of that orange math book, he has stuck on his favorite sticker of her. It's one from back in 2001, when she's just startin' out. Indy Lites. That were when Danica flicked her hair. Dan loves that flick. He loves that sticker. And he loves her. Danica is like all he's ever wanted. He's wrote it all over his school books, his school bag, even his school diary.

"Dan 4 Danica," he's wrote.

Everywhere.

At dinner, Dan tells his folks he's done all his school work, and they can go check if they want. No, they trust him, there's no need to go checkin'. He can stay up to watch TV — at least until the race is over. Dad says he might watch this one too. Dad likes football more, but he thinks that maybe Team Eagle F1 is gonna do well this race, so he might just watch it. Dan knows they will do well. 'Cause Danica is the lead driver.

Dan walks back to his room, opens up the screen on his computer and makes it open the Internet. He goes to the Formula One page. Needs to check them positions again. 'Cause it just seems too good to be true. But there it is—right there on the screen—Danica Walker and Team Eagle F1 made it to Q three and she's on grid number ten. It's the best start ever for a woman in Formula One. Oh man, Dan just feels so proud of his girl. Proud as hell.

He turns around to look at her up on his wall. That poster is the junk! That poster makes him real glad he's a man. He likes it so much he has two copies of it … the wall one and that other one in the cardboard tube. The tube one is ready for that awesome day in November, when he gets her to wrote on it. Danica stares down at him from the wall one. It's from last year, when she were still in IndyCar. She has that pink race suit on, but except it's zipped down, right down, so Dan can see her belly-button. She's on some beach and her hands are up in her red hair, kinda lifting her hair up. Danica has hair the color of a forest fire. Dan loves that color—well, not in a forest fire mind—but he loves it when it's on Danica. But that ain't the best thing about his poster, 'cause under that race suit, you can see Danica's got on a bikini. A black bikini. He can see that gap between her boobies. That's such a sexy place—that gap—and he has dreams about kissing her there.

Them nice dreams, with surprise endings.

Oh man, Dan can't get enough of that poster. Can't get enough of Danica and them pretty green eyes, and them even more prettier boobies. And then... well... the thought of that fire hair... now don't tell no one, but the first time Dan ever bopped off, well, it were looking at that poster. And he's done it a whole lot since.

Turns out Danica grew up in Dunkirk, Iowa, just like Dan did. Her folks' little house were 'cross town, down near the river, real close to Mr. Mack's, where Dan gets haircuts. The Rensburgs came to Dunkirk when Dan were just a baby. Most of his kin still live over in Oskaloosa. Farmin' folks. He has cousins in Nebraska too — and Dan were named after an uncle who died just before he were born — but he's never really met them cousins. He ain't never been to another country, like Iraq. He went to Chicago once, but that were all. No, Dan has only ever lived in the same dumb mud brick house, on the cracked-up concrete of Hay Street. His folks don't have so much money. So he's never done nothin' too grand. Yet.

Danica ain't like Dan. She done a whole mess of things. She would have been a young girl back when Dan's folks arrived in Dunkirk. She went to school over the river in Illinois and her folks moved to Chicago when she were only ten. She like, raced go-karts and Formula Fords and Indy Lites and IndyCars and now she's racin' the fastest race cars in the whole world! And she were doin' it for a U.S team. Yeah, Danica were doin' history. She scored a point way back in Australia. Dan knew gettin' a point were a real big deal in Formula One. Real big. She had scored more since back then. His girl.

He hit control and alt and delete and his computer screen saver came on. **DAN 4 DANICA** it flashed; pink screen, same as her pink race suit; black words, same as her black bikini.

DAN 4 DANICA

DAN 4 DANICA

DAN 4 DANICA

Dan never did figure how they got to make the word pree, when they wrote the word prix. And the British Grand Prix were one hell of a race; even Dan's dad said so, as he turned off the TV and told Dan to get to bed. School t'morrow and it were real late. Dan sure wished they had cable, so they could watch races live. But that weren't gonna happen, not now Dan's dad lost his job. And how were they gonna pay for the plane to Austin for their special big vacation?

Dan lies in bed and looks up at that picture of Danica. He worries about that vacation. Worries like hell. But he feels excited about her race. She made a real bad start. At the end of lap one she were way down the back. But man, she drove so good. On the last lap, she set to racin' that French guy with the real big ears. And she beat him! Tenth place and a point. Dan went nuts. He got so loud his dad said he oughta shut it down, case he woke up his big brother. Didn't Dan remember Dunstan was headin' away again soon?

But what a race! Danica got another point. She has three now. Most ever for a woman. He looks at her poster again. She's starin' right at him. It looks like she wants him … in that way … almost as much as he wants her. It's late, but Dan can't sleep. He needs to bop off. Needs help from Danica…

It's only a ten minute ride in the funny little bus to the Circuit of the Americas. Only ten minutes, but Dan can't sit still. It feels like his head might pop. He's so damn excited. He got that C on a history paper. He done it on Formula One. Worked his butt off. And after all them F grades, he done got a C. It felt like he were in some dream, but when he looked at his paper again, that big old red C were still there. For the first time ever, Dan weren't last in class.

Who's the dummy now?

Momma were so proud, when she seen that paper, she burst out cryin'. Dan seen a tear in his Dad's eyes too, but it got wiped clean real fast. Men folk don't cry in Dunkirk.

'You got yourself a deal partner,' his Dad kept on sayin'. 'You got yourself a deal.'

Dan cried that night too. Hid away in his bedroom and cried. But they was happy tears. Real happy tears. Because that's when he knew ... he were goin' to see Danica.

Dad could only afford to buy two tickets, but mom didn't wanna go anyways. And Dunstan were up in Clinton, sayin' goodbye to his girl, Annie. He were shippin' out end of the week. So it were just Dan and dad, stayin' in a trailer park next to the circuit. But the tiny trailer only had one bed in it. Dan had to share a bed with his dad. Gross! Awwww ... no matter. Today he were gonna see Danica for real.

Friday morning. At the best racetrack in the whole world. First practice were comin' up real soon. Dan's pit pass is in one hand and his cardboard tube in the other. And in that cardboard tube is his Danica poster, just waiting for her.

"Dan 4 Danica," he is gonna ask her to put on his poster.

He knew she would too. And like, once she'd wrote on it, he'd never let that poster go; even when she were World Champ and it got to be worth a million bucks. Never.

The bus takes them down a funny stone tunnel, under the track. Dan hears the sound of engines. His heart is beatin' so hard, it feels like it might bust right out. The bus stops behind a row of long white sheds. There's cars and trucks and semis all over the place. Busy as hell. Race team stuff. So many people. The smell of oil and rubber. Engines screamin'. Dan's so excited, he thinks he might puke.

It's real lucky dad is a big guy, Dan thinks, as they gets a place on the steel fence. His dad shoved other people back so they got a spot. Now they was right near the path where the drivers walk from their trailers to the pits. But Dan soon gets to notice that he and his dad are at the wrong end. The drivers start walkin' away before they get to his end of the line. The two Ferrari guys, the world champ from Germany, that tall Aussie with the big teeth — they all walk past. But not Danica. She's American. Danica won't do that. She'll come along and thank all her fans. Like, Dan's countin' on it.

Practice is real soon, but Dan still hasn't seen Danica.

He starts to worry that she's gone past the crowd, or got in the pits before his dad and him got to the fence. And they only got pit pass for today. Tomorrow they will be out on them bleachers near turn 11. Eatin' a Dog and drinking a soda. Getting' all burnt by the Texas sun. If he's gonna see Danica, it's gotta be today. Then there's a big hullaballoo down the other end of the line. And Dan just knows it's her…

'Danica,' folks start hollering. 'Hey Danica. Over here Danica.'

Dan leans hard on the fence, tryin' to see. He sees a little bit of her white uniform and that fire-colored hair. She has blue shoes on. And she's gettin' closer. But it's real slow. That means she's signin' stuff. That means she's gonna sign his poster.

Oh man!

But he's just gotta keep calm.

Waitin'.

Waitin'.

Oh man, it feels like she's never gonna get to him.

He reaches down between his legs, takes the plastic cap off the cardboard tube and slides out that awesome poster. It's gotta be nice and flat and ready before Danica gets to him, or she won't have time to wrote her name on it. He takes the black pen from his pocket and bites off the lid.

People start pushin' and shovin' as Danica gets closer. Dan's dad protects him from the worst of it, but it's real hard to hold his poster so it stays safe. It starts to get bumped and messed up. Danica is just a few people away from him now. He can hear her talkin', with the same voice like she has on TV. She has dark shades on. So cool. She's shakin' hands and smilin' for pictures. Dan remembers his phone is still in his pocket. He wants to get a picture and all. Show Dunstan and some of the guys at school. But his hands are full with poster and pen.

He feels himself gettin' mad.

'Dad,' he yells. 'Quick, reach in my pocket please Sir. My phone. Need a picture.'

He feels his dad's giant hand push down into the top of his pocket, but Dan's pushin' so hard against the fence that his jeans are pulled real tight. Danica's almost there.

This is bad. Badder'n hell.

He's got no choice. Dan puts his poster on the ground, bends down and pulls out the phone himself. He starts hittin' the screen to make the camera work. But he's gettin' upset now. Makin' mistakes.

Wrong button.

Wrong button again.

He finally shoots one picture, but it's all blurry. Gotta take another...

And that's when Danica turns and walks away.

No.

'Danica,' he yells. 'Danica, please sign my poster.'

But Danica just keeps walkin', like she didn't even hear him. A big muscle-man in a Team Eagle cap puts his arm on her shoulder and takes Danica to the pits.

'Danica!' Dan roars. 'DANICA!'

But it don't make no difference. She's gone. His girl. His perfect girl. Gone. The lines of folks begin to walk away from the fence. Dan sees all them people walk past him, with their hats and pictures and posters, all wrote on by Danica. He sees the little love heart she always puts on people's stuff. He know he should have one of them love hearts on his poster.

"Dan 4 Danica…" and then one of them pretty love hearts.

He looks down to where his poster were layin' on the ground, while he took out his phone. Like, the wind has rolled it out onto the pit lane, where ordinary folks ain't allowed to go. A small guy in orange clothes comes walkin' along, with a trash can on wheels. Dan sees him pick up the poster.

'Hey,' Dan yells. Starts wavin' his arms. 'Sir, please … that's my Danica poster.'

The guy looks up at Dan and makes a face. He shakes his head and shrugs his shoulders. Then he screws the poster into a ball … and he throws it in the trash.

A SINGLE WORD

THEY WENT GLIDING PAST THE GLASS, THOSE VISTAS OF Clinton, Iowa. Familiar streets in monochrome. In time, the views stopped and he heard the hiss of pneumatics; saw the red bricks of the bus station and walls of faces gleaming with patriotic fervor. Silent, gloved applause. The stars and stripes berserk on snow-flurry winds. He looked and saw those faces of freedom, bought by the blood of guys like Captain Tony Walker. But these people didn't know about that. They just didn't know…

They hadn't lived in the dust and the dirt. They hadn't been riding in a Humvee, nerves like glass waiting to be shattered when the earth blew up in their faces. These folks hadn't seen what an IED does to a good man like Tex Walker. They hadn't carried the butchered remains of their friend's leg to a Blackhawk at full power. Felt the dead weight. The warm stickiness of the gore. Smell of burnt flesh. Voices screaming over rotor wash. Phantoms in dark helmets, emerging from a wall of yellow dust to wave a man away. These people didn't know any of that…

And then, in the midst of all that naive jubilation, there she was. Right there, in the same place she'd been nine months earlier. Annie. He remembered the perfume she wore that warm, blue spring day. Fresh, like the smell of the tropics. A last kiss goodbye. The taste of salt on her cheek.

There'd been all those Skype sessions. Sitting in front of a tiny screen, in that plywood box he'd called home. How missing her hurt like the worst kind of hunger. And he remembered the last thing he'd said to her from Bagram. The last question, before he rushed out to board the C-17 home. How it was hard to get down on your knee and still stay in view of a webcam.

Now he saw her green kitten eyes and her favorite blue woollen hat. The dimples when she smiled. Cheeks rosy with the cold. Her silent steaming words. No ... it was a single word ... on repeat.

"Yes," Annie Grainger was saying to him. Answering that question of his; "Yes ... Yes ... Yes!"

OLD "TANKY"
CHANDELLE TX

KAITLIN'S ON THE CORNER

PART 1 — CHAD AND CHANDELLE

THE SMELL OF GASOLINE HELPS HIM TO REMEMBER. It reminds him that things could have turned out so very differently. Maybe he could have been honest with himself. Maybe he could have been honest with everyone else. And maybe he could have been honest with her. There were so many maybes... But you couldn't take time back. You couldn't take that pitch again. You had to play the ball you were thrown. And if you hit a foul, well that was life. Still, nothing stayed the same forever, not even in a place like Chandelle, Texas. Boys grew into men, girls into women, and thriving regional centers could erode away until folks barely considered them towns anymore.

And yet...

Some things did stay the same. There were some women who were never girls, at least not in his eyes. Some women who could make the world spin backwards.

Women with eyes that could bring a young man to his knees. Eyes that would keep him awake at night. There were women with bodies.

That body ... her body.

OK, so she hadn't changed, but Chandelle sure had. Not even highways — iconic, solid, black bitumen — stayed in place forever. And when the truckers and the holiday-makers gave up the famous old road for the straight-line speed of Interstate 40, the old route began to vanish into the land. And as she died, the road took her towns along for a final ride. Yeah, when the highway vanished into the land, and the whole world drove that damn new multi-lane, things really started to change. It wasn't just Chandelle. It happened all the way along the I-40. Slow death in the heartland.

He can remember the time so clearly, even if it was more than thirty years ago. They were starting to build the local sections of I-40 back then — Oklahoma City to Flagstaff. No one in town gave it much thought, except to say it'd be much quicker to drive into Amarillo to buy stuff. They didn't seem to consider that the planners had given Chandelle the slip. A five mile detour into your town mightn't seem like much to a local, but it was going to be too far for travelers, in a hurry to be somewhere better. Yeah, the day the Governor cut that red, white and blue ribbon, that was when things started to change.

Chad Collins remembers that year. The same one they swore in the new President — the quietly spoken peanut farmer from Georgia. And he can still remember a cool night, a few months earlier, back in 1976. He can almost see the flicker of the TV out in the living room and the sound of his father hollering in disbelief.

'He won Texas, Lorene,' Carter Collins kept yelling. 'Goddamn it, the son-of-a-bitch just won Texas. When's this state gonna wake up and start voting the right way!'

The Collins family had always been Republicans. Richie — Chad's grandfather — still had a Nixon sticker on the bumper of his old blue Riviera. Even after Watergate and the resignation, his grandpa refused to take that sticker off his car. He never drove that big old Buick anymore. Couldn't see too good. Couldn't afford the gas bills. It stayed parked outside his retirement home in Amarillo. The paintwork was fading, like that bumper sticker. Perhaps that was just as well.

Chad also remembers a blue and orange Monday morning in July 1977, back when Chandelle was a thriving town of 2,500 people. There were brush fires burning brown on the western horizon. The morning smelt like stale smoke. Soon the day was shimmering. Shining with glare, and the promise of a new Coupe

De-Ville down at Walker's. Dizzy with the heat, and thoughts of spending time with an angel.

Chad ran himself a shower, then brushed his teeth in front of the bathroom cabinet — the one with the mirror on it — and he scowled at those puke-colored tiles that reminded him of fresh cow pats. And once he finished his teeth, he looked closer into the mirror, to see if any facial hair was growing. Maybe there was a little more on his top lip? In the shower, he'd noticed a little more downstairs as well. His voice was going down, despite the occasional girly squeak. It was happening. It was all happening. That was choice! Chad was only three weeks from turning fourteen years old.

He was also running late. Real late. So he jumped aboard his gleaming green dragster and peddled his heart out. He pumped his legs until his face turned the color of rare t-bone, steaming on the grill. He rode down the side of the wobbly tin barn, along the edge of his mom's dead garden, dodging between weedy islands of junk — stuff his dad bought and promised to fix one day, but usually never did — then he bunny-hopped the bike over the yawning dirt gutter his father dug during the last storm season. He was soon riding fast down the black crunching dust of West 4th Street. He was going to have to break the record to make the bell that day.

Chad couldn't remember the last time it'd rained. Not seriously. Even the storm season had been a failure so far. And while it was good to not have to worry about twisters, everything in town was either dying, or dead. The trees along the street were struggling to hold onto their leaves and the grass was the color of hay bales. Dust rolled along the edge of the street, and out from his tires, floating on winds that felt like they'd tumbled straight out of a drying machine.

A few doors down he saw Mr. Barnes sitting out on the front steps of his long white and green trailer. They gave each other a wave. The old guy had to move his stuff into that trailer last year, when a storm took most of the roof off his house. Mr. Barnes hadn't had a job in a long time. He was on a pension. He couldn't afford to pay someone to get up there and fix that roof for him. And he only had one leg—after the other one was blown off in some war—so he couldn't fix it himself. Some of the local folks were pitching in on weekends to help, but without a professional roofer, it was taking them an awful long time. Still, at least in Chandelle, you could rely on folks to help each other out.

Chad took a right when he got to Main Street, at the corner where Bonzo's Barber Shoppe was. Everyone had their hair cut at Bonzo's—even Chad's mom. Bonzo was a crazy Italian man, clown-faced and always happy.

He had a long black moustache that he used to oil to sharp points. He gave the kids candy after their haircuts. Chad refused candy these days. He was no longer a kid. Kids didn't have hair growing on their plums.

On the opposite corner to Bonzo's was the Chandelle Gospel Church. His folks were married at that church, way back in '64 — it stopped his dad from getting drafted into the Army and maybe Viet Nam — but the family seldom went to church anymore. Easter and Christmas mostly. Chad remembers a couple of weddings and a funeral. Bobbing for apples at the fall church fete. Pamela Sandler in the kissing booth at every spring fair. Perky Pamela, with tits like Dolly. Chad'd almost plucked up the guts to do it last spring. Pay two bucks and kiss Pammy. Almost.

Kids had to be careful riding along Main Street back in those days before the I-40. The old highway crossed right over Main and folks were always arriving in town on their journey east or west. There were always strangers who didn't know the local roads. Crazy drivers. Truckers who were half-asleep. Things were always busy in downtown Chandelle — even at the weekend — and Mondays could be especially wild.

Chad rode past the wide glass windows of PJ's Pawn Shop, trying not to look at that catcher's mitt, the one that'd been signed by the '72 Rangers — the first team from Texas to win a major league game — and the one his father said they couldn't afford. So he looked across to Mr. Cumquat's grocery instead. And he wondered if there might be work available sometime soon, maybe even this afternoon. A few hours' work for a few dollars, or a soda, or some candy. More than anything though, Chad wondered about her! His angel. Going into that store meant seeing her.

'Later man…'

Chad rode down across the intersection with Third, past the official tan brick of the County Offices on one side of Main Street, and the white and red stone of the Texas General Bank on the other. Mr. Michie had opened up his electronics and hobby store early that day. Chad could tell by the little battery-operated plane out front. A blue plane today. It was flying on the end of a piece of fishing line. Flying around and around and around. There'd been a red plane until last week, when Chuck Weinberger cut the fishing line and set it free. The guys never did find where that plane landed.

Chad slowed down when he came to the next block. Eyes wide, ready to stop, even though he was running late. But Walker's Autos still had their doors rolled down and the new Coupe De-Ville was hidden away from view. So Chad peddled harder again, swinging to the left into East 2nd, past the bright red roof of the steak restaurant, and he was almost collected by a long white Ford pickup. He gave a cheeky wave to the shouting pickup driver, and then saluted the town water tower — Old Tanky — standing on his four gangling insect legs, *Chandelle TX* painted in bright blue letters around his gleaming white tank. Chad was now pedaling so damned hard, it felt like his legs might melt.

Late now.

The school bell was ringing as Chad shot across the wide dusty shopping center car park — already half-full — into Madden Ave and up into the grounds of Chandelle Junior High. He clamped on the rear brake of the dragster and left a satisfying, inch-thick skid mark on the concrete next to the bike shed. It stretched for more than six feet.

'Let's see McDowell beat that,' he whistled as he slipped his front wheel into one of the racks, collected his bag and ran like hell.

The bell rang again, but the usual feeling of dread wasn't there today. Sure he had a history test this morning, which he hadn't studied for. And, no doubt, he'd have to face a few hours with the fat-bitch substitute teacher, but who cared. Oh yeah, he sure was looking forward to the day. Well, he was looking forward to the end of the day. The afternoon. The grocery store. He felt sure she was going to be there.

Her…

There was no doubt in his mind — today was going to be the best day of his life.

PART 2 — CHAD AND KAITLIN

That kid hater with the purple hair makes me tired just looking at her. I think it's because she never stops moving, even when she's standing still. Now she's wobbling away under that filmy brown dress, while her hippopotamus arm scratches up the list of stuff for homework. She's in love with homework.

Goddamn Ms Jones.

She came as substitute for Miss Johnson last year. And then she just stayed. She bought a little house down on West 2nd and now she substitutes every time a teacher is away. I don't get her at all. I mean, I don't even know what "Ms" means? Or how you say it.

'Muz? Mezz? Mizz?'

Does it mean someone who is half way between a Miss and a Mrs? Kit Renshaw told me it was code for "dyke." Maybe that's right. Would girls go for her? Man, I don't know.

Anyway, what I really don't get is why someone wants to be a teacher when they hate kids so much?

But she does it. She don't stop. It's like nothing else in the world matters to her. Nothing but school. I even remember the day after the new President was voted in—all that did was give the old hag a new homework idea. We had to write a ten page report on the Presidents of the United States—Washington to Carter. Who can think of ten pages worth of stuff to write about Presidents? Today she's dishing out the homework for math—she's taking Mr. Homan's class this week—and it's two pages of compound fractions. I mean, it's cool, I can do math in my sleep, so I barely take any notice. My eyes turn back to check the clock on the white brick wall. It's almost time. The best part of this day is about to start.

It's frustrating. Days like this seem to go so real slow, but we're almost there. Every second that clicks past gets me close to seeing that shining new Caddy, and the most beautiful chick in the world. I can see her now. In fact I can see both of them. Her leaning on the hood, in a wet t-shirt and tight denim jeans. Washing my brand new Caddy for me. It happens every time I close my eyes…

At three-thirty the bell finally rings. We start shoveling our books into our bags.

'I want to see those answers first thing tomorrow please,' Ms Jones chatters, fluttering her purple eye lashes like the pink-ass monkeys the circus sometimes brings into town. 'And I mean very … first … thing.'

'I mean … very … first … thing,' a voice squeaks behind me. It's a damn good imitation.

I have to bite down on my jaw to stop myself laughing. The old hag has super hearing. Doing an impersonation of her is a suicide mission—especially at this time of the day.

'Mr. Broman,' Ms Jones barks. 'You can spend another fifteen minutes in class now, starting your fractions.'

'Oh Ma'am no,' Broman whines, now a lot less of a smart ass.

'Thirty minutes Mr. Broman. And not another word, or we'll make it an hour. I have all afternoon.' She turns to the rest of us. 'Everyone else may leave,' she says grandly, like she's the Queen of England or something.

I'm tempted to turn around to Mike Broman and say "tough shit", but that's not a smart idea. I can't afford to be stuck here doing math homework. I've got places to go and things to see. New cars to smell. Beautiful women to look at.

It's only a seven minute ride home from school, but it can take much longer if I ride up Main Street and stop in town first. That's the plan today. I'm in no hurry to be home. There's a gas fire wind blowing from the south, out of Mexico and straight up Main. But even with the wind at my back, I can't seem to ride fast enough. So I rise up from the seat and start pumping my legs on the pedals. Feel the familiar burning in my legs. Thoughts of what's about to happen. The dragster rocks from side to side until my bag starts trying to jump off the sissy bar. Dust flies. It still ain't fast enough.

The new Coupe De-Ville has arrived at Walkers. I see it from a block away, sitting out on the forecourt of the garage. It's a real beauty, with gleaming chrome, burgundy paint and that soft creamy vinyl around the rear third of the roof. The six rectangular head lamps and that big silver grill. The Caddy badge. Beautiful. I've been bugging old man Walker about it for months. Every day I'd say to him: "when's the Caddy arriving?" Every day he'd say to me: "sometime next week!" And then he'd laugh.

But it's here now. And it looks even better than it did in the magazines.

I slide my bike to a stop, drop it on the dirt and walk towards the garage, right up to that beautiful new car. It has that smell—the new metal and vinyl and paint smell that cars have when they're brand new—kinda like chemicals, but nicer. Our family had never bought a new car—never had the money—so the new car smell always felt like it was part of someone else's world. Exciting and kinda forbidden, like a place I might never get to go myself. I look through the glass and inside. This one had red seats with white trim; the Caddy logo is stamped into the velour; thick red carpeting; air conditioning and even a cassette tape player. This is the sort of car I'm going to buy one day—even if it ain't brand new—once I make myself a stack of money.

'Don't you go putting greasy marks on my new baby,' a deep voice rumbles.

I turn around and see Mr. Walker, kinda snarling, with that mouthful of huge dark orange teeth he has. Teeth like empty beer bottles. He's not angry or anything, just being his usual self.

Mr. Walker is a pretty old guy. He was in the war with my grandpa, or so mom said. The two of them fought in some place called Gwaddal Canal, or something like that. I think that's in England, but I'm not sure. Was there even a war in England? I know the Krauts bombed there, but did they invade? Or didn't mom say they were fighting the Japs? They never invaded England. Man, I can't remember. And I'm not gonna ask Mr. Walker, that's for sure. People in Chandelle don't talk about the war—especially not the last one. You know, the recent one, the one in Viet Nam. The one some folks say we lost. Anyway, unlike my grandpa, Mr. Walker never retired to Florida. He stayed in Chandelle and kept right on selling cars.

'You know I can read fingerprints, don't you young Collins?' he chuckles. 'If I find any of yours, I'll have you washing down cars for me for a week. You know my rules, look, but no touching.'

'Yes sir,' I say, walking back out of his garage, picking up my bike and pushing off. 'Thanks for letting me take a look sir.'

'Y'all come back when you have some money,' Mr. Walker yells after me. 'Better still, bring that cheapskate father of yours.'

I don't reply.

I point the dragster up the gentle rise of Main Street and ride past rows of stores. Familiar stores. Stores that have always been there. That means I know them all. Chandelle Hardware is where my dad is always buying knick-knacks; something to fix something else he broke. Red Tex Steakhouse is where we sometimes go to have a sit down meal. They do the best curly fries at Red Tex. I don't like vegetables too much, but I love those curly fries. Dad says the Bank of America owns most of our stuff—and I don't really understand what he means by that. Michie's Electronics and Hobby sells cool models and kits and stuff, but kids are now banned from going in the shop without their parents, after some of the guys from school got caught stealing stuff. That's why Weinberger and his pals started cutting the little stunt planes free — it was like a protest. There's the pawn shop of course, but I can't even look in the window now without seeing that signed Rangers mitt. I worry someone else might buy it, before I save enough money to get it myself. And once it's gone...

But I ain't worrying about any of those other stores today. Today, there's only one place I'm going to visit. Today I'm riding towards paradise!

Mr. Cumquat has owned the grocery and take-out store on Main Street since forever, well, at least since I was a little kid. His real name isn't Cumquat, it's something from Checko-slavakia and no one in town can say it properly, so everyone just calls him Ivan Cumquat — or Mr. Cumquat if you're a kid. Truth be known, I don't really know what Cumquat means neither. Someone told me it was a fruit, but that don't sound right. I thought it might be part of a woman's body. Clint McDowell showed us a sex magazine in the school bike shed last week. His brother's in the Army and he brought it home from Japan a few weeks back. I'm sure someone said there was a photo of a Cumquat in that magazine ... you know ... part of the woman's pussy? Now every time I say the word, I think of pussy. Every time I go into that store I think about pussy. But there's another reason for that...

Mr. Cumquat's grocery is a blue steel building that used to be a delicatessen. Out front it's kinda long and sloping and there's a big green canvas awning stretching out from the door. On the front wall is a school chalkboard, where Mr. Cumquat writes his daily specials. He's selling double-scoop ice cream cones for the price of a single scoop, but today only. I lay my dragster on the edge of the sidewalk, out of pedestrians' way, and head for the door. No ice cream for me today, even though it's hotter than hell.

Stella is Mr. Cumquat's Golden Retriever. Every day she lies on her yellow mat near the door and wags her big bushy tail to welcome each customer. Mr. Cumquat moves her mat through the day to make sure she's always in the shade during summer and in the sun during winter. She's thirteen and doesn't like to get too hot or cold. I gently pat her silky head as I walk past. She gives me a big lick and that feather-duster tail starts to go thump-thump-thump against my legs. I pat her again and she stares up at me with her sad brown eyes. She's a beautiful girl. I'd like to have a dog like Stella, but my mom is allergic to all the hair.

I walk into the store, out of the heat and the dust, and Mr. Cumquat gives me one of his funny gummy-bear smiles. He's a round hairless man with piglet skin that's always shining with sweat. On hot days like today, when he's cooking fries, or flipping burgers on the grill, you'd swear he was going to explode. And if you ask him if he's OK, he will always say: "never got this hot in Prarg." I'm not sure where "Prarg" is, or how to spell it. I guess it's in Checko-slovakia.

'Hey boyo,' Mr. Cumquat says, his squat little arms held wide, like he wants to give me a hug. He calls all kids boyo, even the girls. Adults, well he always calls them "boss."

'Hi Mr. Cumquat,' I say, never daring to get to close, in case he carries out his promise and actually does hug me.

Guys don't hug other guys in Chandelle, except when they score a rare touch-down or hit an even rarer home run. I mean, I can't ever remember getting a hug from my dad, even when I was a little kid.

'You wanna do job?' Mr. Cumquat asks.

I smile. Nod.

'I sure do.'

Mr. Cumquat sometimes asks me to do a few little chores for him, in return for a few dollars, or something from the store. He might ask me to ride a delivery for a customer on my way home, stack the shelves, or sweep out the floor of the store.

'That's my good boyo!' He starts waving those little piggy arms of his, almost knocking his little copper statue of Jesus off the counter in the process.

He told me he bought that statue from a man on the Saint Charles Bridge in Prarg. Again, I don't know where that really is, but ever since he's owned that statue, Mr. Cumquat says he's had good fortune. I'm not so sure about that. I never stare too closely at that Jesus statue. The face kinda gives me the creeps. It has little sparkling eyes, and when Jesus stares at you...

'OK, so how'd ya like a free soda?' Mr. Cumquat barks. 'Giant size!'

'OK...' I reply, cautious, wishing he was offering cash, and wondering what the job might be. Still, it was a real hot day and a giant soda would sure go down well. If I'd known what I was about to see — and who — I'd have offered to do it for free. Man, I'd have paid him...

Mr. Cumquat always has a few boxes of stuff out in the back corner of the store. He hides stuff under the big old staircase, which takes you up to the little apartment where he and Mrs. Cumquat live. The boxes he has in there today are kinda big and Mr. Cumquat has a bad back. The store is already full of stuff and there is another delivery truck due anytime. He wants me to move some of the cartons outside, open them up, and help him stack the shelves, and then we'll make room for his next delivery. It sounds easy enough, but those boxes are huge, and he's got a lot of 'em.

I wrap my hands around the first carton. Turns out it's not very heavy at all, but it is wide and kinda awkward, and my fingers scarcely reach around. So I sort of half-lift and half-drag it out to the glaring furnace behind the store.

Out back, behind each of the Main Street stores, are a series of small courtyards. I don't really know why. Anyway, Mr. Cumquat's courtyard has a small plot of grass — dead — and a couple of white metal chairs. When the summer sun lights up that little courtyard, and when there ain't much wind, it gets so hot in there I swear you could cook burgers on the ground.

So hot…

I almost drop the box. I almost trip over my feet. I stand and stare and try to swallow, but my throat has suddenly turned very dry. I hoped to see her, but this… this… well… this is better than I could have possibly imagined. It's like a dream. One of those dreams that give you a rude shock in the middle of the night. Lying on a long pink beach towel, in the middle of Mr. Cumquat's courtyard, brown and baking in the sun, is the most beautiful woman God ever put on the earth.

Kaitlin.

Kaitlin is Mrs. Cumquat's niece. Her people own a hog farm about five hours south of here, just outside Austin. She quit senior high last year, which caused a big fight with her folks. So she kinda ran away. Mrs. Cumquat was worried about her running away further and getting herself into trouble, so she gave her niece a safe place to stay. Next year Kaitlin wants to go to night school in Amarillo, to learn hairdressing. Until then, she's staying here with her Aunt and Uncle, in that tiny little apartment above the shop. She helps out with running the place, earning some money. Today is her day off. That makes sense; because I tell ya, Kaitlin ain't dressed for work.

She stirs at the sound of dragging boxes. Looks up.

'Oh, hi Cutie,' she says, rising up onto her elbows and flashing those perfect white teeth; ones with a little gap in front. Her orange bikini falls open a bit and I find myself entranced by the golden valley between her tits. Perfect tits. Tits so close to me... I feel kinda giddy. I lean against the carton, trying not to look stupid.

'Hey,' I reply, trying to be cool.

I must look like I'm tuckered out. I can feel the embarrassment burning my face. Ketchup red. Stupid. I hope she didn't notice me staring at her tits.

'They look heavy,' she says, nodding in the direction of the staircase.

There are cartons everywhere. I pulled the bottom one out first. Not too smart. The rest of them have spilled out and into the courtyard. I'm such a moron.

Still, they're only potato chips, so they're not heavy and the contents shouldn't be too badly damaged.

'Oh, they're OK,' I say. My voice kinda chirrups out of my dry, swollen throat, like a strangled fart. 'Not too heavy.'

'Strong and cute huh.'

'Guess.' I'm really glowing now. Glowing and aching. Aching and tingling.

I don't really remember when "those" feelings first came over me — those dizzy, scared, excited feelings that start in your head and quickly move to your chest, and then other places — but I'm sure they were when I first saw Kaitlin. Things start stirring down there. It doesn't get hard, but it feels like it could at any minute. I feel like one of those spring-loaded toys that you can buy over at Mr. Michie's, the ones that burst out if you don't latch them down exactly right. I swallow hard and try not to stare. Try not to get excited. It's impossible.

Kaitlin rests on her elbows, her chin in her fingers, and she smiles. Her blonde hair tumbles down onto her bare shoulders. She has her hair flicked back near her ears, like Farrah Fawcett wears it. Her eyes are wide and beautiful. Eyes the color of springtime in Texas. Golden-green eyes. She gets dimples on her cheeks when she smiles. And she has that body! The curve of her nude back glows pink and brown, shining in the angry sun, shining with tanning butter. For a tiny moment I imagine my fingers running down her spine, inside the seam of her bikini and onto that perfect ass. I imagine touching her "down there", while I kiss her on those dimples. It's like one of those pictures in McDowell's magazine — and then the clothes start coming off.

It's too much.

I almost lose control of myself at this point. It starts to go hard. That oily stuff starts to ooze out the end. I can feel moisture down there. I must look like a complete jerk, standing there with my stupid red face and my cock throbbing while I try to hide the growing wet spot on my school pants. Meanwhile, I desperately try to think of something intelligent to say to the most perfect chick that ever existed. Once again … Mission Impossible…

Mr. Cumquat comes to my rescue.

'Hey boyo,' he yells from just inside the doorway of the store. 'There are still lotsa boxes in here. No soda until you moves and unpacks all of them.'

'Sorry,' I say to Kaitlin, my voice solemn, like my leaving might be the saddest thing she'll have to deal with today. 'I have to go and move these other boxes.'

'Have fun,' she replies, reaching around and undoing the catch of her bikini top before lying face down on the towel again.

Watching her do that … oh man … I'm so horny, it feels like I might vomit, or explode, or perhaps both. I have to do something. I rush to the stinking toilet between Mr. Cumquat's place and the store next door. Slam the door. Unzip. In less than twenty seconds I start winding off the last few squares of toilet paper left on the roll. I wipe it dry.

A week goes past. Pretty busy week. Mr. Cumquat has chores for me every day. I enjoy a full week of Kaitlin sightings. Tonight Mom wants to call the doctor, because I'm off my food. I don't say much. My stomach is twisted like a bike chain. I feel completely hopeless. Can't hardly breathe. I try to reassure her it's nothing, but how do you tell your mother the only sickness you have is totally desperate horniness? She feels my brow for the hundredth time.

'He doesn't feel too hot,' she calls to my father, who is entrenched in front of the TV News.

'Course he's not. Boy's fine,' my father bellows back. 'Leave him be and come and listen to this socialist screwball talking about health care.'

I put myself to bed early. Soon, the evening burns with velvet darkness. Our creaking old house is alive with news. My father is actually singing out in the living room. Drunk and partying. He's convinced Carter's done it this time. He keeps yelling out stuff. Little chants and stupid songs with no tune:

'Oh yes, America will soon realize how dumb they were.

America will soon eat their hat.

America you were so damned stupid.

Voting in a Democrat.'

I don't take much notice. In the humid darkness of my bedroom, I start to party too. I create my own little fun park. All I need is a little privacy, a glob of spit and some imagination. I work fast. In less than a minute I'm lying warm and sticky under the sheets. Feeling awesome…

I learned how to do that last year. No one taught me or anything, I just started playing with it until something amazing happened. I've been giving it a regular workout ever since — under the shower, in the toilet out back of Mr. Cumquat's store, but mainly in my bedroom. With my father making such a fuss out by the TV tonight, there's no way my folks would have heard me, even when I yelled out "Kaitlin" right at the end. I always worry they'll catch me doing it, or that mom will notice the starchy stains on my boxer shorts or bed sheets when she does the laundry. If she has noticed, she's never said anything about it to me. I'm real happy about that. Talking about that sort of thing to your mother would be worse than dying. Way way worse! Not that it'd stop me. I don't think anything could stop me. As soon as I'm alone, my thoughts turn to nothing but sex. It's always sex. And it's always with Kaitlin.

Kaitlin is all I think about in the daytime as well. Kaitlin in her orange bikini, Kaitlin in those tiny blue denim shorts she wears, Kaitlin in her tight pink sweater, Kaitlin in nothing at all. That last one requires a little imagination, but not much. You have no idea how much I want Kaitlin. I spend hours fantasizing about her, and how one day she'll be mine. I know she's a few years older than me, but my parents are five years apart—so what's the big deal? And I can tell she digs me too. Don't ask me why, I can just tell! And that's why I can't leave myself alone. I saw her again today—serving behind the counter in the store. Mr. Cumquat was running an errand and then Kaitlin and I had that store to ourselves. Oh the things I wanted to do in that store. Things with Kaitlin. I lie in bed reliving the scenarios. Then, after about an hour of Kaitlin fantasies, I'm ready to spank the monkey all over again.

It's Saturday before I see Kaitlin. Five days without seeing her feels like forever. Five nights alone with my hand. I think about taking her photo somehow—to help the imagination along a little—but I wonder if I could ever pluck up the guts to ask her. Probably not. I'm such a pussy!

Anyway, today, most of the town is out on Main Street for the Foundation Day parade. I park my dragster under a bush on West 3rd and walk down to Main to see what's happening. I find a space behind the barriers and watch the fire department go rolling past; the lights and sirens going on the shining red engine and old Walt Cunningham waving from the driver's seat, wearing that stupid old black helmet of his.

Big deal. Who cares!

But then...cometh the goddess. She's why I rode down to the parade today. She's why I'm here.

'Ah yes,' Mr. Michie says over the P.A, because aside from owning the electronics and hobby store, he's like the town announcer. He was a Marine Sergeant in Viet Nam and he's got a voice like you wouldn't believe. It scares me a little. 'Please welcome the 1977 Chandelle Cheer Squad.'

Right on cue, a line of girls comes marching out onto Main, behind the fire engine. They're in short green skirts, long white boots and red sequined tank-tops, with cowgirl frills. They're shaking enormous green and red pom-poms, though not really in time with each other.

This town hasn't fielded a decent team, in any sport, for at least ten years, but somehow we've found ourselves enough girls to be official Chandelle Cheerleaders. And this year, of course, Kaitlin is one of them. The wolf whistles start as the girls go marching past, with their high kicks and their flashing pom-poms.

'Give us a "C",' the girls start chanting as they move down the street. 'Give us a...'

'Come here and I'll give ya some "C",' a tall trucker beside me hollers. 'C'mon, haul it over here darlin'.'

I notice who he's calling to. Patsy Podmore smiles and winks in our direction. She's wobbling and swaying down the street, looking like a wild hog in white boots. Her gargantuan tits sway like caveman clubs inside her tank-top. Those things move so much it looks like they might tear themselves free at any second. She waves her pom-poms at the trucker. Smiles and winks some more. Patsy has more teeth than brain cells, and she doesn't have all her own teeth either. She's easily the dumbest person I ever met—and in Chandelle that's sayin' something—but she has something the men in town can't resist. They line up outside her house like buzzards on a bighorn—especially after pay day. Clint McDowell reckons they're payin' her for "it." I don't get it. Why would anyone pay to do it with Patsy? Why would anyone do it for free with her, now that I think of it?

But what I do get is Kaitlin. You'd pay Kaitlin — I'd pay her every penny I had. She's towards the middle of the marching line. And she's dancing twice as good as any of those others. I stare, afraid to blink in case I miss a single thing. And as she bounces and swings, I notice that she's not wearing a bra under that tank-top. Don't get me wrong, I'm not an expert on women's bodies or anything. Apart from those magazines in the bike shed, I've never even seen naked tits, but I can tell what Kaitlin's look like, just from staring at her tank-top. They're not like Patsy's wild white wobblers. They are firm and brown and beautiful. I can see the perfect, sweeping shape of them. The way they move, firm, but soft. I can see the pointy part of her nipples. Oh man, all I want to do is touch them. Play with them. A lot...

It's a hot August night, just another night for me and my right hand. It's been three weeks since the Foundation Day parade, but I still can't get Kaitlin — and that red tank-top — out of my brain. And I don't want to either! It's like my eyes took a picture of her that day; now all I have to do is close them and there she is, bouncing along in my own private movie show. Those perfect tits, with their shape and that brown cleavage, and those silver dollar nipples pointing out all loud and proud. I can imagine myself kissing them. In McDowell's sex magazine, there was a picture of a guy rubbing the head of his piece on a girl's nipple, then sliding it between her tits. She'd made it all oily in there. How hot is that! And in the next picture the girl reached down and ... oh, the thought of Kaitlin doing that to me ... the feeling of her perfect lips on my piece...

It happens again. White noise, muscle cramps and a warm, wet lap.

Man, since that parade, I'm averaging two a night, and sometimes three or more. The record is five. I'm starting to freak out. What if I'm sick or something? I mean, like a pervert. And what if I run out before I'm old enough to get laid? Dave Nolan told me a guy only has a certain number of shots stored in his balls. So how many shots does the average guy have? And once you've used up your allowance, do you get any back? Crap! I'm gonna have to do something about this soon, 'cause if I'm about to shoot myself dry, one time has to be for real. And that one real time has to be with Kaitlin.

That night I begin to hatch a plan, right there in the warm afterglow of another jerk-off session. I need a sure-fire strategy to make her mine. Every so often I lose focus. I have to keep reminding myself that this isn't silly and that anything is possible. I'm sure Kaitlin doesn't have another boyfriend, 'cause you hear about stuff like that in Chandelle. Everyone knows everything in this place, well almost. And I think Kaitlin digs me. I mean, I'm fairly sure she does. God, I know I dig her. I've got a red-raw piece to prove it. But I don't have long. She might leave town soon, or get picked up by another guy. I gotta do something more than just fantasizing. I gotta make my move.

So I fight off the sleep, wipe myself sort of dry, and start working on my plans. Good plans. Great plans. Perfect plans. And after an hour or so planning, when it all gets to feeling too exciting, I spit in my hand and start spanking that dirty monkey all over again.

My plans come together on a hazy Saturday afternoon when Main Street turns to liquid and the tall steel street lamps seem to wilt down towards the ground. My father's off playing golf in Blairsville—'cause he'd play even if the world was ending—and mom and I have the house to ourselves. I've been watching mom turn maroon and exhausted as she wrings water out of the freshly-washed drapes onto our dead back lawn. Then, after I help her hang the drapes out on the line, I jump on my bike and head down to Main Street. Today is as good a day as any. Today's perfect.

Mr. Cumquat and his wife have gone to Amarillo for a few days to see their son's new baby, their first grandson, a little Cumquat. But that doesn't mean the store shuts. Mr. Cumquat always opens for a few hours on a Saturday and since he's not there, Kaitlin has to look after business. For the first time in a month she'll be in the store on her own. This is the moment I've been waiting for. And, despite all my meticulous planning, I don't mind telling you, I'm freaking out. So much could go wrong. If I blow this … no … no, I ain't gonna blow this!

I slide the dragster out onto West 4th. The tar looks waterlogged under the hot August sun. Everything shimmers and sweats. Everything boils. I'm burning up too, but that's nothing to do with the heat. In a few minutes I'll be there. In a few minutes my life could change forever.

I take my time, riding gently and letting the southwest wind push me along. The roads are empty, well almost. Chuck Hurley's grey Chevy pickup drives past. The dust swirls out the back and the meat hooks clang against the tray. Chuck's ugly black hunting dog roars at me with angry wet foam, before returning to the three wild hogs bleeding under its feet. For a few seconds, my dad's aftershave is overwhelmed by the sickly sweet smell of dirty dead hogs. And I just keep riding.

Even Main Street is pretty quiet today. Not many cars around. But there is a big blue car parked out front of Mr. Cumquat's store. I know that car; a tricked blue Camaro with race tires and a red eagle decal on the bonnet. Down the sides, orange and red flames lick the paint work. Metallic paintwork and baby-buffed chrome. It's the sort of car that attracts highway cops like flies. Just by looking at this type of car, well you can tell the owner is a jerk. And he is. He beat me up once when I was a kid — for nothing. I worry that he might be in the store. He could screw everything up. But I can't stop now.

I pat Stella and walk inside, out of the blast furnace heat and into the dusty store. It's a little cooler inside, but only a little. There's a tall silver fan whirring away on one side of the store, bothering the small magazine stand and sending the hot dusty air into a frenzy. Apart from that humming fan, the shop seems deserted. There are no frying smells, nothing on the grill.

I shuffle up to the counter, lean against the red formica and I give Jesus a confident wink. Things must be going OK, if I can look that spooky statue in the face. I decide not to call out, 'cause that just seems uncool. Kaitlin's obviously out the back. Maybe she filling out an order or doing some papers or something. I've already forgotten about that crappy Camaro and its dip-shit owner.

Then I hear her voice. It's muffled, like she's wrapped up in a blanket or something. There's giggling and then more speaking and I realize she's talking to someone else. Maybe she's on the phone? Mr. Cumquat has one out the back. I wonder how to get her attention.

Damn it.

It feels like my plans are starting to go bad. My fingers ball into fists. I just have to keep it together here. So what would a cool bloke do? Click my fingers like the Fonz? No! Then I remember that James Bond movie from TV last week. When he wanted to get a girl's attention he just kinda cleared his throat. It was polite and cool at the same time. Perfect!

I wait until the store goes really quiet and I clear my throat. It comes out high and choked, like a little kid with marshmallows stuck down his windpipe. Nothing happens and so I try again — deeper, smoother and louder. There's shuffling in the back room. It sounds a bit like boxes have fallen over or something. The commotion lasts about five seconds and then I hear whispers and the squealing of door hinges and then she appears — Kaitlin.

Her hair is all over the place, messier than I've ever seen it before. It looks like she's just jumped out of bed or something. She's wearing a pink sundress, the one with buttons down the front, except that half of the button aren't done up properly. Her bra strap hangs loose on her right shoulder and her neck and cheeks are flushed pink, like the color of raw frankfurters.

'Hi,' she says, kinda out of breath.

There are no pet names, no smiles and it feels like she doesn't want to see me.

'Are you OK?' I ask sounding exactly like a scared little kid.

'Huh? Oh yeah, I'm fine. I'm just feeling the heat I think. What do you want?'

It's the rudest thing she's ever said to me. I'm thrown. I'd rehearsed a dozen suitable lines for this point, but they've all vanished. I just stand there and feel the sweat soaking into the huge love heart card I've got tucked down my shirt. That damn card cost all of last week's allowance.

'What do you want?' she repeats, sounding really annoyed.

'Ummm…'

My James Bond routine is long gone.

''Cause I'm shutting up soon. Can I get you soda? Some candy? What?'

I've never felt more like a little kid than I do right now. Sodas and candy — what the hell? Didn't she know what I could do to myself after dark? The things I'd seen in that magazine? My fantasies? That wasn't kid stuff.

'Why you shutting early?' I bark. 'Mr. Cumquat wouldn't like…'

'Hey, why don't you take off shrimp.' It's a man's voice, choked tight with husky, smoky passion. He sounds like a miner or a trucker. Someone who's been sucking fumes and dirt too much. But he sounds somehow familiar.

He flashes out from the store room, swinging on the door frame like some hairy-ass baboon. Jerry god-damn Hewson. The owner of that blue Camaro. I hate that prick, with his hard square face, and scraggly beard. His eyes are red and bloodshot and his hair is long and brown, like a lion's mane. He's wearing a button-up flannel shirt that's unbuttoned and his denim jeans are tight and bulging. I notice he's got one of those wet patches like I get. It's obvious — he and Kaitlin have been … I can't believe she could be so dumb.

'It's OK Jerry,' Kaitlin croons. 'He's OK.' She gives me a flat smile, like the one Ms Jones gives me when I solve a math problem. It's the kind of smile people give each other because they have to, not because they want to.

I look at Jerry for a second. I hate his guts — even more than when he beat me up that time. The lunatic inside me even contemplates a suicide mission to try and beat him up. But I'd need a weapon, and there's nothing on the counter that looks suitable, except the statue of Jesus, and I don't think that'd be a good idea.

'What are you doing here?' I growl, sounding way tougher than I am.

Jerry swings away from the door frame and falls against the counter. He pumps himself up and down on the edge a few times, like doing push-ups. His orange arms flex and shine.

'I'm Kaitlin's friend. Now why don't you buy your little bag of candy and get the hell outa here.'

'C'mon Jezz,' Kaitlin giggles, running fingernails in S-shapes along the muscles of his arm. 'He's a good kid.'

'Yeah,' Jerry mumbles, his jaw clenching and his eyes burning. 'You're a good kid'.

He reaches for her butt and pulls her to him. He kisses her once, twice and then they interlock. Their faces seem to melt together. And when I see her tongue slide into his mouth, all I can do is bolt outside.

Stella kinda yelps with surprise, as I crash through the door and into the sunlight. Angry tears start to flow. Can you believe it—fourteen years old and I'm crying. I rub my arms over my face while my trainers pulverize the dust. I kick the tires of my bike and scream with rage. Then I point the dragster down the grey dusty sidewalk and jump on. I peddle like hell. And I vow to set this right.

'This ain't over,' I say to myself. 'This just ain't over.'

Familiar words start sprinkling through my head, firing my heart.

"We shall prevail," the lunatic voice inside me keeps saying. "Don't you give up." "We shall prevail."

Part 3 — Chad and Kaitlin's Corner

The smell of gasoline still did it to him. Made him remember — things he mostly wanted to forget. It was the year they re-elected the President. The black Democrat from Chicago. And despite all those years of paternal influence, he quite liked Obama. Not enough to vote for the guy, but enough. And, despite a solid reelection, the Democrats didn't win Texas. That would have made his dad happy, if the old boy had been alive to hear the news.

It was an indecisive scrapbook of a day, in that town with scarcely 250 people. There were showers on the air and scoop pictures of next year's Chevy Coupe leaking on the internet. He didn't expect to see that car locally anytime soon. Old man Walker died back in '84. The dealership that still bore his name sold Korean cars now, and was close to going bankrupt. That was no real surprise — most of Chandelle was in the same boat.

The bathroom tiles were still that horrible cow-crap color, but the face in the crazed old mirror was a revelation. Most mornings, the owner struggled to remember who it was. He had turned fifty a few weeks ago. The silver hair and the laugh lines around his eyes. The way his mouth kinda curled at the edges when he smiled. Damn it, he was starting to look like his father. In fifty years, he'd managed to go nowhere, beyond adopting the face of a man he'd never really learned to love.

He decided to clear his head. Take a walk around town. He sauntered out the side door, under the carport, then out along the edge of his wife's happy little garden. His father's mountains of junk, random pieces of machinery, the old engines and gearboxes were long gone, replaced by neat garden beds and lines of roses. It was good to see his mom's garden looking like it was supposed to look. It was also good to be able to walk around the yard without worrying about stepping on a Prairie Rattler. He'd seen a few of them hiding in the backyard over the years—heard them rattling mostly, since they were so good at hiding down in the grass and weeds—and folks were always gettin' bit when he was young. He still remembered the day Buddy Burnett was bit by that big old rattler down the end of the street. That was back in '79. Buddy's dad killed the snake after it bit his son. Nailed it to his front fence to show everyone.

That damned thing was almost two foot long, thick like your arm, with a big head like an arrow. The paramedics had to take Buddy to Amarillo. He almost died.

He stepped over the crumbling council drain and onto the black crunch of West 4th street. The storms had been heavy recently. Though the twisters had given them a miss, there'd been plenty of soaking rain and the trees along 4th Street were the nicest he could remember. Elms and Cottonwoods with thick canopies of leaves. Lawns heavy with lush green grass; grass that hadn't seen a mower in years; grass growing high against houses threadbare and falling into ruin; grass where a rattler could lie up for weeks and never be seen. Only two families lived in his part of West 4th now. His only neighbors were talking about leaving too. Retiring to Amarillo. His home town was a tenth of its original size—and disappearing fast.

He walked steadily, listening to the sounds of his boots on the loose crunch of the gravel. A few doors down from his place, he passed old Mr. Barnes' house, now a rumble of grey lumber and rusting tin. His long thin trailer, now more green than white, started sitting at a crazy angle after the wooden blocks holding up the front right hand side rotted away. The government had moved the old guy off to a veterans' home in Dallas a couple years back. No one in town knew if he was still alive or not. No one checked. People didn't seem to care about each other so much anymore.

You seldom saw many people on Main Street these days. There were few reasons for locals to loiter and even less for visitors. A street with few active tenants — unless you counted the dealers, waiting to offload some more crystal meth to the sunken-eyed kids who sat on their skateboards among the weeds. PJ's Pawn shop was still there. PJ Junior sold a few old wares and souvenir kitsch to the occasional tourist who stumbled off the interstate, hoping to experience the heartland, or get directions to where they really wanted to go. Most days the store was dusty and silent. That lad had to be the most optimistic man in the state.

There was hardly anyone else still open along Main. The steak house and Allen Michie's hobby store had been vacant for decades — boarded windows with graffiti tags sprayed onto them — and the bank closed its doors about a year after the interstate was finished. There was an ATM in the front wall, until the night Bobby Atherton tried to bulldoze it out of the brick work with his Dodge Ram. It meant you had to drive to Amarillo now if you wanted to get cash out. Mr. Cumquat's grocery was put up for sale after the sweet old guy finally dropped dead in '99. A buyer still hadn't been found.

It was like watching a loved one wilt away — living in this dying town.

Further down Main Street, Walker's Autos were still trading, but even they were closing down at the end of the summer. He walked past a single row of small SUVs with "Everything Must Go" signs stuck on the windshields. Old Mr. Walker worked there right up to the last minute of his life. He had a massive heart attack, just as a lady customer was about to sign on the dotted line for a new Continental. The paramedics arrived, but they couldn't get his battery restarted. Still, rumor is, he got the woman's signature before his ticker finally gave out. Mr. Walker always made the sale. Tough old dude…

The big white water tower was still there, of course, but the state and county were arguing over who should pay for his restoration, if indeed restoration was warranted. Residents aside, no one seemed to agree that the tower was of any historic value. As far as the folks in charge were concerned, Old Tanky was little more than an eyesore. The letters on his white tank had all but faded and those long white insect legs were streaked with rust stains. One decent storm, he figured, one storm with a twister, and the whole damned thing was going to come smashing down.

He walked around to Madden and then back up town until he found himself on the corner of East 4th and Main. Though the Gospel Church was still there, the congregation was struggling to pay the bills. The gas station on the corner was closing and the barber shop had long sold out. Still, it wasn't all bad news. There was one ongoing business on that corner, where Bonzo had once cut everyone's hair. One business was shining in that fading little town.

Hers…

Yeah, Chad Collins still lived in Chandelle, Texas. He'd never left. He was married now, with three grown-up kids who all lived away from home. Chad married a girl called Kate, but not the one he used to visit at Mr. Cumquat's shop. As for the other Kate—Kaitlin—well, fate sort of took her from him.

Was that what it was? Fate?

Really?

Then, as he walked along to the corner of 4th and Main, Chad thought back to Veterans' Day 1977.

It had been a cool silver day. A sky angry with glare. A heart filled with teenage rage. There'd been another parade down Main Street. But there were no cheerleaders this time; no pretty girls in long white boots and tight tank tops. This day, people marched in uniform and somber remembrance. Kaitlin didn't march in this parade. No, she was too busy making out with a hairy-ass baboon.

Jerry Hewson lived with his dip-shit family in a dip-shit house out on the end of Chester Street. The Hewsons were supposed to be part-Cherokee, or so they told everyone and anyone. Folks kept them at a distance. They were violent and angry people. They were always getting in trouble with the cops. The father was a drunk. The mother was always getting beat-up, either by her husband, or one of the many men she had affairs with. But by Veterans' Day 1977, she had changed her life. She moved down to Austin, and married a trucker who had converted to Islam. Pattie Hewson changed her name to Fatimah Yusuf. The last time Chad saw her, she'd covered her whole head with a black scarf. He thought he saw peace in her eyes.

Jerry's sister, Lisa had recently run away to New York or someplace like that. Chicago perhaps? Dancing in strip clubs—that's what folks said. Either that or whoring? The elder brother had been doing regular jail time for assault and battery. Drunken rages. He narrowly beat a manslaughter charge, but the local cops and judges all knew his name. It was only a matter of time before the dumb-ass did something really stupid and got life—or worse. He decided to join the army instead. They sent him off to Basic up in Oklahoma and found out he could drive heavy machinery. Eventually they shipped him off to Germany with the 2nd Cav. No one was in a hurry to see him back.

So there were three of them living at that dip-shit house: Jerry, his father, and that shiny blue Camaro. The hairy baboon always parked that car in the same place, right out in front of the house, under his bedroom window, so he could look out on it, and nearest to the street, so the rest of the town could see it. Jerry loved that damn car. And now he loved Kaitlin. Chad wasn't gonna let that continue...

When Chad arrived at their place, on Veterans' Day 1977, Jerry and Kaitlin weren't there. No one was. Jerry's father served in Korea — and he had a son serving overseas — so he was marching. Chad knew exactly where Jerry and Kaitlin would be — upstairs, above Mr. Cumquat's shop, making out while she was supposed to be watching the counter — and that made him madder than hell. Mad enough to do something really stupid.

Jerry was eternally working on that damn blue Camaro. He was always out there with it, fixing something or washing or waxing it. That day, Kaitlin obviously had surprised him mid-way through some task. The two of them had left in a hurry. Why they'd not taken the car, Chad had no idea. Didn't care either. Jerry had forgotten to properly lock down the hood. Chad noticed that as he'd ridden past on his bike. So he rode home as fast as his legs would peddle. He had a plan. And he had to get a few things.

Chad used to like watching his dad tinker around with machines. He learnt stuff. He knew about cleaning greasy, oily machines with a little bottle of gasoline and a flannel. Knew gasoline was useful for many things. Yeah, Chad learnt stuff alright. He knew where the brake fluid reservoir was in an engine bay. He knew how to put a tiny cut in a brake hose and how to drain some of the fluid out of the reservoir using a big old plastic syringe. And he knew gasoline in the brake system was a bad thing. All that friction and heat… Maybe the damn car would burn. Maybe Jerry'd take it driving that afternoon and smash himself up.

Good.

What he didn't consider was that Jerry might take someone else for a drive in that car. Or that the "someone else" would almost certainly be Kaitlin. Chad never thought about that. If he had, he might not have done the things he did. He might not have had to live so long feeling guilty. Because Chad would never dream of hurting Kaitlin.

The news began to filter into town on the evening of November 12th, 1977. Whispers between neighbors. Phone calls floating the wires like rumors on the wind. By morning, the papers had picked up the story. As had the TV news in Amarillo.

The Randall County Deputy was called to an auto accident out on route seventy. A cold rainy night. A car had left the road on a sweeping bend, not far from the Reservoir. No apparent reason, it just went straight ahead. The cops assumed it was speed and the wet road. They recognized the car, and knew the record of its owner. Not to mention his dirt-bag family — plenty of driving fines on the files for those punks. Plus the kid had painted those ridiculous flames down the side of that Camaro. Thought he was Johnny Rutherford or something. Every time that fool went out on the road, there was an accident just begging to happen. No surprises that it now had. But then the front wheels had burned. That was unusual. Even though he never recorded the details in his notebook, the Deputy did wonder about that.

There'd been a passenger in the car, an eighteen year old Chandelle girl, and she had two broken legs and serious head injuries. She was flown by chopper to Amarillo for treatment. Doctors said she was in a real bad way—it was only 50/50 that she'd make it. The driver of the car, Jerome Marlon Hewson, a twenty-one year old, also from Chandelle, was pronounced dead at the scene. The Deputy made sure that detail was recorded. It almost felt like a result…

It had taken Chad days to get the gasoline smell out of his hands. He didn't sleep. He didn't eat. He flunked all his end-of-year exams. And more than three decades later, that oily sweet smell you get when you pull into the driveway of a gas station—well, that still made him feel guilty. He should have confessed. He should have gone to the cops. But he didn't. And the fact they blamed Jerry Hewson for his own demise, helped Chad keep his secret. The cops were just as happy to see that asshole gone. Case closed. The guilty were free to live out their lives.

Sort of…

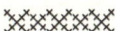

Chad pushed the thoughts away again, and walked up and onto the sidewalk on East 4th. Walking across the corner of 4th and Main always made him nervous. It was her corner. And she still didn't know about the car. She didn't know anything.

Kaitlin was still in town. Though she lived out in Blairsville, she still worked in Chandelle. After the big accident, she had stayed in hospital for well over a month. The break in her right leg was so bad the doctors had to put a metal plate inside, to help it mend. Three decades later, she still walked with a slight limp.

After she was released from hospital, Kaitlin spent some time with her sister Debby up in Nebraska. Debby was married to a big-time preacher — Chad could hardly imagine Kaitlin living with a preacher — but when that didn't work out, she went back to her folks on the hog farm near Austin. Eventually, Kaitlin came north again. She went off to night school in Amarillo and got her hairdressing certificate. Then she came back to Chandelle, bought Bonzo's corner barber shop and turned it into her own salon.

Now, Chad found himself standing by that little pink shop again. Standing and shaking. Sweating palms. He was there again — frozen beside "Kaitlin's on the Corner." But he was determined this morning would be different. It'd been long enough. Yes indeed. Today would be different.

'Different…'

Kaitlin never married. Told folks she'd never found Mr. Right. The consensus around town was she'd gone dyke. Cut her hair short and everything. Maybe the car wreck — that bump on the head — well maybe that screwed with her brain. But Chad knew the real reason. At least he told himself he did. Every once in a while, he would go past her salon and their eyes would meet and at least one of them would wonder about what wasn't, but should have been. About days and nights. About that warm, eye-closing feeling of riding the fringes of ecstasy. But a glance and a thought was all it would ever be. There was too much guilt. Just too much guilt. Until…

Today Chad didn't just sneak a glance into Kaitlin's shop. He didn't have an appointment. He didn't have a damned clue what he was doing, but he walked right inside. And it wasn't until he was in the middle of that corner salon, with the door buzzer whizzing and the smell of hair products thick in his nostrils, that he realized what he was trying to do.

After all these years?

God, they were in their fifties. Surely it was time.

He stood there surrounded by walls made of mirrors and something pink. He was everywhere in that salon — a happily married man, standing in a place he should never have gone — he was everywhere and completely alone. He felt the jabbing of guilt in his gut again. He was about to leave. And then she came in.

'Can I help you?' Kaitlin asked.

She had hardly changed. She wore her hair a little

shorter these days, a little blonder perhaps, but she was still there, in that face and those eyes. The same voice. And that body. Kaitlin had sure looked after herself. She exercised a lot — though at first it had been to build up the strength in her damaged legs — because she loved the rush it gave her.

A rush … Oh yes…

It'd been thirty-six years, he was married to the most wonderful girl and they had three great kids, but, at least on this corner of a dying town, and in one man's gut, nothing had changed. Kaitlin still drove Chad Collins crazy.

'Haircut?' was all he could say.

'Appointment?'

'No,' he said, his head falling forward, turning to leave.

'It's OK. I don't have anything for a while. I can always fit you in.'

When Chad looked back up, she was pointing in the direction of the chair. A smile on her face. Those dimples.

That smile.

His smile.

'C'mon cutie,' she said, in the voice from out at the back of Mr. Cumquat's shop. 'Tell me how you want it.'

An hour can change a man's life. Chad Collins knew that now. An hour and everything can be the way it once was — or even better.

Kaitlin didn't cut Chad's hair. She didn't shave his cheeks and the back of his neck. She didn't wash and rinse and blow dry. Kaitlin made love to him. He sat in that chair and felt the tiny erotic stinging of her nails as she worked her fingers through his hair. The cool steel of her scissors against the nudity of his neck. And the heavenly vista of her face. How she held his chin gently in her fingers as she ran a razor over his sideburns. How she stared into his eyes with hers, and how those eyes were the same color as the cottonwood trees in early fall, and how those soft pink lips were the most perfect things he'd ever seen, and how his arms began to ache as he dreamt of reaching out and running his fingers through the golden shimmer of her hair, even as she ran her fingers through his, and how he kept thinking that kissing Kaitlin would be the most perfect thing a man could do. He sat back in that chair as she did his fringe and he felt the heavenly warmth of her breast against his ear as she tilted him back towards her body to finish the work. He floated in the presence of her. The coconut spice of her body spray carried him to places beyond anything he'd experienced with any other woman. Even his wife.

'My wife…'

'Sorry?' Kaitlin said, tilting him forward again and gently dusting the hair away from his face.

'Why aren't you somebody's wife?' Chad asked.

She turned him around in the chair, and looked into his eyes. Oh yes, she stared at him with those perfect yellow-green eyes until he had to look away.

Burning. Burning.

'Because cutie,' she purred, 'the right guy never asked.'

She reached forward and kissed him on the forehead. Slowly. Warm and soft. He shivered and began to levitate as her hands touched his ears; as he stared down into the dark paradise of her cleavage; as he watched her taking a deep breath; as his heart stopped. She was going to say something to him. She was going to say it…

Yes.

Say it…

'Now,' Kaitlin whispered sexily.

She was finally going to say it…

'That'll be twenty-five dollars. And next time make a damn appointment.'

BOOKSTORE CONFESSIONAL

You think it's about time I confessed, confirmed what you've known for years. Thanks for that. And yeah, OK, I know I'm self-centered and self-absorbed. I understand I'm an egotist. I'm painfully aware that I'm single and I'm embittered. My tolerance levels—never really high—have now lowered to almost zero. I messed up once and I'm never going to forgive myself. But then it's just easier to blame everyone else. Yeah, OK, enough hints … I get all that stuff … I'm forty-two and I'm depressed. You don't have to keep reminding me.

Partridge and Partners adopted the open office model the week after I turned forty. A bad combination for a guy like me: too many people, too loud, too irritating, all sitting too close to the office asshole. My days became a concoction of stress headaches and cramping jaws. At my last check-up, I blew the doctor's blood pressure machine off the scale. He gave me one of his red-faced lectures. Now he has me out and walking each lunch break.

Well, he had…

I gave up the streets after a week. Dodging mind-less, meandering crowds on the sidewalks and sucking carbon monoxide seemed hardly conducive to improv-ing health. I'd go back to the office like a torsion bar. Like a coiled spring. One stray comment and…

I tried Gateway Park — change of scene and all that jazz — but the sight of sweetheart-snuggling secretaries was too much for me. I'd been condemned to the bunker of singleness after all. Am I being too melodramatic?

Yeah? Well screw you.

Anyway, I kept trying. I found a seat down on the river, and that was a little better, until the warmer weather arrived and the she-joggers started bouncing past, slic-ing me in two with those perfect lycra bodies. I lasted another week. I don't know what horniness does for blood pressure, but I'm sure it's not good.

But still you kept nagging me about taking a break. It's like you were my doctor's little messenger. No let up! So I went looking for another sanctuary — mostly just to shut you up. And eventually I found *The Nest*.

I went back there today…

The Nest is down on Chestnut. It's the last of the old-style bookstores, with every vertical space occupied by shelves; twists and turns and hidden corners; titles you could no longer buy anywhere else; a café with chrome-legged tables and seats with tea-dyed cushions; the comfortable smell of fresh book paper and coffee grounds; checkerboard floor tiles and walls papered in old movie posters; '*It Happened One Night*' meets '*Casablanca.*' It's a blessing—a slice of old-style retail in this instant gratification, single-click world we've made for ourselves. I go there a lot, not to buy books—I'm way too cheap for that—but as an escape. It's a chance to slow down, to stop, and to work on that blood pressure.

Today it's where I find Sandra Walker—formerly Michie—in her white blouse, blue jeans and red heels. I guess you remember me mentioning her? You should, I did it often enough. Sandra's my girl. She's the only one that has ever—but never—been.

We met on the West Coast, vacationing when we were kids. Though we lived on opposite sides of Chicago, we always kept in touch. We used to write all the time, sharing stories of school machinations and teenage lament. When we got a little older, we started circling around the sexual mulberry bush, but we never dared take a branch and climb. No—that's not really true—I never dared. Sandra climbed alright. She climbed high. And she left me behind, standing on a soggy carpet of shed mulberries, and hating myself. That was when we started losing touch. Eventually she married and had a couple of kids—which still amazes me—and she settled down.

Sandra's husband was in the Air force—based out at Whiteman—something to do with stealth bombers, so no one says too much. They bought a little house over in Warrensburg, started raising their two little girls. I moved here to St Louis, to work for Partridge. Bought a little red stone place about ten miles out of the city and I lived there on my own. Yeah, OK, you don't have to remind me. I know it's my own fault.

Sandra and I still used to catch up occasionally. A drink, on those rare times she found herself in the city. We'd sit and make small talk. I'd drink too much and burn. I'm sure she noticed, but she'd never say anything. She hadn't come in for a while now. Too busy I guess. Or was it me? Anyway, she's here today. And now I suppose you want me to do something about it…

She's in the mind, body and spirit section, eyes deep inside some hardcover with swirling rainbows on the jacket. I loiter on the other side of the book stand and watch. Age hasn't been kind to Sandra—but who am I to judge—she's lost as much weight as I've gained. Her face is sallow and concave. The blonde wash can't quite hide her silver roots anymore, but her hair does look better now she's let it grow down to her shoulders. The boy-cut never suited the shape of her head. It reminds me of the time we gave each other freak-show haircuts. Bright green and shaved. Do you remember the pictures? Sandra and Todd... we were so stupid back then...

The simple white blouse seems conservative, compared to what I remember her wearing—back in the days when she insisted on being called "Sand"—but I can still see those dark areolas through the material. Bras were never Sandra's thing. Clothes were optional when she was Sand. The things I'd seen of her. Seen, but never touched. She has always been perfect to me. Even now.

She looks up. There's a microsecond of processing, and then a smile.

'Oh my God,' she says, sliding the book back onto the shelf and floating around to my side of the book stand. 'Hello stranger! I wondered if I might bump into you in town.'

'It's a big town,' I say, because I'm dumb like that.

We embrace. It feels familiar, but different. We're sure not twenty years old anymore. But there's still a spark. My hand sinks deep and warm into the curve of her back. I've always loved the way she presses her hips into mine when we hug. Sandra always lit the fuse. That's the truth of it—right there. It's always been Sandra…

'What are you doing in the city?' I ask, still buzzing a little.

'Angie and Trix are on camp this week. Matt is on deployment yet again, so I thought I'd make a day shopping in the big city.'

'Wow, OK, so did you drive yourself this time?'

Sandra never liked driving—certainly not back in her "Sand" days—said it was choking the lungs of the earth.

'I drove to Big Bend and caught the Metrolink from there. It's not so bad. Took me a few hours, but hey, I enjoyed the quiet time.'

I want to jab her about polluting the atmosphere, but I let it go. Who cares?

'Have you eaten?' I ask instead. 'There's a great little café…'

'I was going to get something later, but do you feel like it now?'

Yes I did. I really really did.

I was lying on my back. Sweating. Shivering. Rushes of self-hate and desire…

Hate and desire…

Hate and…

The feeling, the ache, of wanting something so badly, it took away your breath. Jaw muscles burning. Fists shaking white and numb. Down through the dark maze of pine needles I could hear the soft sound of bay waves breaking onto sand. A bird started shrieking.

What the hell was wrong with me?

What kind of guy walked away, when it was being handed to him on a plate? Seriously—who did that? Two beautiful things. It was the ultimate fantasy. The thing young guys bought dirty magazines to gawp over. The type of stuff they tell lies about doing. But not me. Oh no, I had it right in front of me. I had it for real. No fantasy. No lies. And I walked out. I went and slept on her balcony, all by myself. I left the two of them in her bedroom, open mouthed and half-naked. I can still remember the looks on their faces.

Amazed.

Amazed—there's a word for you. Do you like that one? OK, how about appalled? Shocked? Frustrated? Stupid? Lame? Regret is my favorite—capitalized, italic, bold and underlined—***REGRET***.

That night would haunt me for decades. Those two beautiful girls would revisit me in countless dreams; tropical night sweats in the middle of winter; staring at writhing, moaning internet screens; having lunch in a bookstore.

They're playing Springsteen in the café. Songs I've grown to love. Songs of the Heartland. She orders soup and I get the same. I hate soup, but it seems rude to eat anything more substantial in front of her. And yeah, you don't have to remind me, I can do with something light.

'So,' she purrs, 'you still working for those Partridge bastards? '

'I know … I know … the enviro-terrorists. Yes, I am unfortunately.'

'Todd, why don't you get out? Retire early? You have money. Go and write that book you always said you wanted to write. I mean what the hell do you owe them, Todd … after all those years?'

'Don't tempt me,' I murmur.

Again.

She smiles. Goose pimples when her fingers touch mine.

Our soup arrives. Two uninviting bowls full of grey-green broth and a knob of sour cream, served with slices of crusty bread and a scroll of duckling-yellow butter. Sandra scoops off the sour cream, dumps it on her bread and leaves it. I mix my cream in, butter my bread and take a bite. It's doughy and warm; melted butter and nice feelings. For a moment the world goes out of focus and when it comes back, I realize she has a button undone on her blouse. I'm staring straight down there. She notices. She smiles. The button remains unfastened.

'Hey,' she says, eyes sparkling and knowing. 'Remember that weekend out at Fiddler's Point? You know, back in the eighties, when you came to stay at the little place I was renting on the lake?'

'Umm, yeah, kind of,' I lie.

'Yeah, sure you do, my friend Sasha was staying over as well.'

'Do you still keep in touch with her?'

'No. I mean, not for years. We had a falling out after I met Matt. She thought people in the service were all war mongers. You know…'

'Just as well she never met your Dad.'

Sandra stops. She stares down at her soup. Starts making slow circles with her spoon before raising it up and taking a sip. I close my eyes. Toes balling in my shoes until the cramping starts. Yes, I know, I'm an idiot. You don't have to remind me. I'm a stupid, insensitive idiot.

Sandra's dad was a Marine. Allen Michie did time in Vietnam — the siege of Khe Sanh no less — and he was kind of a hero of mine. Won a Silver Star. He retired not long after he came home from the war, moved south and opened a hobby store in small-town Texas, somewhere near Amarillo. He and Sandra's mom died in a car accident just after their only child went to college. That was back in the eighties, when Sandra rebelled, became Sand, and tried to take me along for the ride. I couldn't do it. I loved her folks like my own parents. Doing those things with their daughter, in the way she wanted, well … well it just seemed disrespectful. I tell myself that a lot. It doesn't really help.

'Anyway, you remember that weekend?' she asks again.

'Sort of.'

She looks into my eyes and smiles. She knows when I lie. Always has.

'Do you ever think about that? I mean, what could have happened?'

I bury a hunk of bread into my mouth. Give myself a few seconds reprieve. Why the hell was this coming up now? After all the times we'd caught up. Why now?

Why not…

'Hmm?' One of her fingernails starts tickling the loose button on her blouse, making tiny plastic clicks.

I can feel the blush roll over me like a rogue wave, washing my neck and face in blood-warm radiance. Sweat starts tickling my brow and top lip. I feel briefly nauseous.

'Of course I do,' I finally whisper. 'I think about that all the time…'

'Wow … really?'

I nod, head wilting like some dying flower. I catch my blurred reflection in the glaze of the tabletop.

'You wish it happened … that's it, isn't it … my God, you regret saying no.'

She's smiling now. Her hand grasping and pulling at the neck of her blouse. Maroon rosettes on her neck. Kind of breathless. Excited, embarrassed, or exasperated?

'Maybe … y'know … maybe if it'd just been you,' I stammer. 'I mean, I didn't know Sasha all that well…'

'Hah! You know I thought it was about me. All this time. Do you remember me offering you and Sasha my room, so you could be alone with her?'

'No, I honestly don't remember that part.'

'But she didn't really dig you. She wanted to be with the two of us. She was going through that whole sexual discovery thing…'

I nod again. Take a mouthful of soup. Almost choke trying to swallow it.

'I can't believe it,' Sandra says, jovial and way-too-loud. 'You wanted me that night. After all this time. Hah! I can't believe it! Oh wow! This is so great!'

A couple at a nearby table begins to eavesdrop on our conversation. A pair of silver-haired vacationers, dressed in checks and white shoes, eating club sandwiches and flipping through their book purchases. The woman gives me a disapproving look, her little red dolly

.B. ALLEN

lips puckered, like she's just stuck her tongue into a grapefruit. The man shakes his head as he chews, open-mouthed with a baseball of grey meat. Their judgment feels like tracer fire.

But, somewhat surprisingly, I really don't give a damn.

Yes, I know what you're thinking, hearing all this stuff—my conscience or my invisible friend, or whatever it is you actually are—you think this will be good for me. It's been over twenty-five years and I've finally found a place to talk this stuff out. I finally found a way to exercise a little of that Catholic guilt. Maybe Sandra and I can meet again. Meet here and talk some more. Maybe now I can move forward. Now I've taken a step. Maybe this can be my own little honesty space. I can invite other people around for a chat. All the people I've loved and loathed. The people I've cheated and wronged. You think that maybe this can be my own personal sanctuary.

Welcome to Todd's Bookstore Confessional.

"THE REACH"
MISSOURI RIVER SD

ARCHIE'S REACH

THE OLD WOMAN AND DROWNING

DROWNING IS EASY. SO EASY, ANY FOOL CAN DO IT. When you drown you are numb and swollen and hopeless. It's like sinking into the green belly of the deepest river you can imagine. Staying underwater for so long you don't remember which way is up and which way is down. Drowning's like the temptations of life. Slipping down into something deep and dark and warm and inviting, before you realize it's too deep and too dark and you don't have a prayer of getting back out.

Yes. The old woman is sure that's what it feels like. She should know. She's tried to drown often enough. Came close to doing it so many times.

'So close.'

Yeah, any fool could drown. Any fool except her. Sometimes she wonders if she's not even good enough for that. Even drowning was too good for the likes of her. A failure at everything in life ... even death. She wonders about that. And she wonders if she's really as old as she looks. Or half as old as she feels.

'Lord, have mercy.'

This morning is like every other morning. The old woman wakes and the old woman rises and the old woman trudges through her day. She tries to do life, but most days she finds herself frozen, staring at the luminous face of the river. She stares at the swirls, eddies and reflections of someone else's heaven. She sits like a totem, wide-eyes transfixed by the glow of the water, until someone or something comes along to remind her of current times.

Today a pair of small brown ducks comes whistling overhead, their wings twisting on the morning air. Whistling feathers at dawn. And that's when it all comes back to her — this life and those memories. Memories always seem to find her; her limbs splayed and her body vulnerable. Memories were like men. Most men. That's when she remembers how close she came to really drowning. In a place no one much cared about.

She remembers life upstream, in South Dakota. Life on a lumpy green oval of grass. She remembers an aluminum box and broken windows. Life in a little cluster of trailers. She remembers junked cars, a pair of faded Appaloosas, a Rastafarian Billy Goat and folks who knew about keeping themselves to themselves. They were the days of drowning. The days of loneliness and loss. They were days of malignant regret. The days of the Reach.

THE REACH

Knuckles rapping aluminum made an awful sound. Jolting and sharp. The same sound you heard when one of those big bastards slapped you on the face. It'd only been a few months since the last one. No wonder I was still jumpy. And this place felt even less safe than the others. Grey's Reach: a swollen finger of land, wrapped in a tourniquet of the Missouri. Twenty or so trailers. Piles of junk. An animal or two. That was Grey's Reach. Not that anyone here used the full name of the place. It was always just The Reach.

'I come from down at The Reach,' folks would say—if they were prepared to admit it.

The Reach was down at the end of a skinny red dirt road, where the river took a huge bend on itself and almost lassoed the land. So really, the Feds had put me in a dead end. That didn't seem too smart to me. And since when did aluminum trailers become suitable as safe houses? Priority budgeting. That asshole Reagan. But who the hell was I to argue? I was in no position to do much of anything at all. Not now. Not after all I'd done. These people owned me. Everyone owned me.

Except me.

There was knocking again. Louder. A young man's voice. A familiar accent. Bluegrass slurs. Southern twang. And it was the sound of a man unhappy to be seen outside my trailer. A man in a hurry to be let in.

I opened the door to a crack. 'Yeah?'

I saw a hand and a brown wallet. I checked out the I.D — as if I could read at that time of the morn-ing — then I opened the door and let him in. But I really shoulda dressed properly first. I was only wearing a t-shirt, and if I bent down in front of the guy, half my ass would show. Did show. He noticed right away. I saw his eyes go wide as he walked up my stairs. I saw the look on his face. That hungry, dumb-ass grin. He liked what he saw. Wanted a piece of it. OK, yeah, I guess I'd always had a good body — even though I did nothing to look after it — and that was something. The only decent card I had in the pack. And yeah, I used to use it to my advantage. Still did. I could tell I had this guy under my thumb already.

It used to feel great, y'know, having that hold over men. Still does — kinda. Once it was like the best drug ever. It was the ultimate power. I knew I could break the hardest cat. Just a look. Just a movement. Undoing one button ... and they were mine. Even the dudes at the top of the tree weren't immune. I could make them do just about anything I wanted. There are some names I could tell you. Maybe one day I will. These fat cats would pay me. They'd pay to be with me. Greenbacks to worship in the temple that was my body. And the more they wanted, the more they paid. It was like being a goddess or something. They laid their cash at the feet of my altar. Can you imagine what a trip that was? Especially for a girl from a hick Texas town. My body made me someone. A player. I used to like that.

But now ... damn it ... now my body was about all I had. And I kept using it to get what I thought I needed. But before you go rushing off to judge, maybe you should put yourself in my shoes. Maybe you should have grown up where I did. Consider all those opportunities life gave you, but didn't give me. But no, you wouldn't even entertain the thought, would you? You'd probably run a mile rather than spend a minute as me. And I knew it was a fleeting thing. So what was I gonna do when I lost my body as well? When the power of it faded? Would that thought scare you? It used to scare me...

'Hey,' the guy grunted, as he stepped inside. He looked down to see where he should wipe his shoes. That was some kinda joke! My floor was dirtier than the dirt outside. But this guy was a total dope. He was much less certain of himself, now that he was inside, and on my turf. Inside, he knew the rules didn't apply.

'You alone today?' I asked him.

'Yeah! Crocker's s'posed to be with me, but he's got stomach flu or something.'

He said it like I knew who the hell Crocker was. I probably did, but couldn't remember right then. And I didn't care less. I knew what coming alone meant. The so-called secret code. If they came in pairs there were rules. So they almost never came in pairs. A few of the gung-ho ones did, but not the rest. They made deals with each other. They flipped a coin. The loser was dropped off in Springshore, to kill a few hours in a coffee shop or a diner. And the winner came out to see me.

'Ain't there rules for that sort of thing?' I said. I wanted to see if I could rattle the guy. 'Y'know, single male alone with a female witness?'

'Probably,' he said, with another goofy grin. His face started blushing. Hands shivering. 'So do you want me to go?'

'No,' I said, remembering who I was and why he was there. My goddess days were fast running out. I needed him and his buddies to keep me alive. 'Not after you've driven all this way.'

He cleared away some of my stuff from the bench by the dining table. Took a seat. Took off his shades and put them inside his jacket.

'Where you from honey?' I asked him.

'Grew up in a little place not far from Louisville.'

'I remember Louisville.'

'Mmmm. Hey, you got coffee?' he asked. 'Kinda thirsty and tired.'

I had a little left, some sugar, but no milk or cream.

'Can't do it white,' I said.

'That's cool. Black and sweet does me fine.'

'I'll bet it does.'

He went really red at that point. Another idiot grin. That was when I noticed how young he was. Damn, he still had zits on his cheek. Peach fuzz on his top lip. Cherry boy.

I made him a coffee, but didn't bother making one for myself. I never could drink coffee without milk or cream.

'Thanks,' he said, giving me that goof-ball smile.

There was something about him. Something moved inside me. He was goofy-cute. Like one of those little kids back home; the ones who were always getting beat up by the big kids. Maybe that's why he became a cop. To get back at those kids. I liked that. So I sat on the opposite bench. Leaned forward, letting my shirt neck fall open. Showing him some cleavage. It'd become a reflex. And anyway, he wasn't a bad-looking kid, compared to some of them.

He was kinda Californian, for a Kentucky boy. He had a blonde sweep of hair and a really bad orange tan — one of those tans they sprayed on you in a booth. I could see he worked out, even though he wasn't naturally big. He'd obviously spent a long time in the gym, trying to sculpt out some sort of body shape. He'd done OK. He filled out his jacket nice, and he looked good in his plain white shirt. Plus, he seemed nice enough. He'd started out all cocky — like they usually did — but he was polite enough. And then he'd gone all shit-scared nervous. I must admit … I found that kinda sexy.

'So, how's things been going?' he asked, blowing on his coffee.

'OK.'

'No sign of our boy?'

'No, thank God.'

'Last I heard he was picked up in Vegas. State boys. Some sort of drug thing. I never heard how it ended up. Maybe this time we'll put him…'

'… he'll get off,' I snapped, sitting up and pulling back on my shirt. 'He always gets off.'

'Yeah. Anyway, he's a long way from here … twelve hundred miles … so don't worry about it. You'll be fine.

He can't possibly know where you are.'

I didn't reply. This guy knew nothing. God, how long had he been out of Cop School? A week? Had my status dropped that low already? Was I so unimportant now they'd send rookies out — and let them come out solo? It didn't bode well for the future. Still, at least he didn't have the nerve to ask for the usual. I'd led him on pretty good. So maybe I had the kid all wrong...

But then he did...

'Anyway,' he said, face broiling, like a Baytown furnace worker. Sweat on his brow. His hands started shaking again. 'Crocker was telling me that you sometimes... y'know... kinda as a favor for us coming out this way... do, y'know...'

Of course. Crocker. I suddenly remembered him. He was a tall white-bread asshole from Memphis. Curly red hair and freckles — all over him — and sweet shitty breath, like something out of a cow's ass. Another dirty, low-life bastard; thinking that was part of the deal; thinking it was allowed; thinking it was expected; because of who I was; because of my background. Actually, most of them were the same — these guys who came out solo. But I really thought this kid was different. Hell, he didn't even look like he'd popped one out yet. A monkey-faced, spray-tanned try-hard. He was like the uber-virgin.

I smiled. Gave him the eyebrows; 'Really?'

'Yeah, you know … we are putting in a lot of extra hours for you.'

'For which you get well-paid.'

'Not as well as you'd think ma'am.' He smiled, this time kinda dumb-like. He'd turned redder than hell. 'Plus, I'm not married or anything. So, y'know … it wouldn't be no sin…'

'Well, in that case…' I slipped down off the seat, bent forward and reached for the fly of his pants. I put on the mask. Went back into character again. It just happened so easily. Like I was on remote control…

He started to shiver. I mean, really hard-core shivering, like he had a chill or something. And he started breaking into a sweat. A heavy sweat. I mean, God, I thought his spray tan was gonna start melting. There were guys who had that kind of reaction. It was always pretty creepy.

'You OK honey?' I asked, playing with him for a second.

'Yeah, sure thing,' he replied, trying to pull himself together. 'Must be the caffeine getting to me or something.'

'OK, well y'know there are rules to this thing,' I said, my fingers teasing the hem of his boxers. 'No arguments or I'll ring your boss. And since this is your first solo visit, this is all we're gonna do…'

I told him the deal. Then I did it as fast as I could. I took off my shirt and coughed a few globs of spit onto my right hand. Then I pulled down his boxer shorts and did it. And I looked out the window while I did the trick. Yeah, OK, I dug out some of my best lines — told him how hot he was making me.

Yeah … yeah … yeah.

Biggest I'd seen.

Felt so good.

Wished I could have done more for him, but there were rules.

You know, the sorts of things girls like me are supposed to say. Or maybe you don't.

The kid was a firecracker with a real short fuse. It didn't take him long. He left almost straight after I finished. Didn't say a word. He just zipped up his pants, kinda nodded, all goofy-like, and then he left. Then I stood over my little kitchen sink, turned on the faucet and washed the mess away from my hand and between my fingers.

He wanted it to go in my mouth, then on my face, then my tits, but I refused each time. There were rules. He didn't know nothin'. He was mine. So he did what he was told. We found a compromise. The t-shirt went back on before he blew. It was going to need a wash now, but hell, it already was filthy. I certainly wasn't

letting him go on my chest without something covering
it. Not until I owed him something. And maybe not
ever. Maybe I didn't feel so sorry him.

'Dirt bag.'

I turned off the faucet, dried my hands on the bottom
of my dirty shirt. They were all just low-life dirt bags.
You should have heard the noise he made when it happened. For a minute or so, until he came, he was full of
tough-guy bull. Porno talk. As I looked out the window
he started ordering me to do things. I ignored him. I
told him the deal. Threatened to stop. Then I put on
my t-shirt and kept going. Suddenly, he went kinda pale.
He shrieked like a little girl. He put his hand over his
mouth to muffle the sound — like he might have done
if his momma was in the next room, listening to him
jerking off — and that's when it happened. He had a
lot on board. Poor fool. He shot it all out-of-control,
like a little kid trying to fire a double-barrel. Made me
real glad I hadn't agreed to what he wanted in the first
place. Not when there was that much in store. I never
did get used to that taste. Not without a whiskey chaser.

A double.

I took off my shirt and threw it on the floor with the
other dirty laundry. It landed stain up. His gelatinous
shots were starting to soak into the fabric. Yeah, didn't
that just say it all? That was the sum of my worth to

these people — a few globs of goo today and testimony at some time in the future — I was worth less than shit. Not a real person. Not to them. None of them. And once they had my statements, then what was I left with?

'Damn it.'

I found a pair of pants that were semi-clean, pulled them up, sat on the bench and lit a cigarette. Felt dizzy and alone. Used and abused. I was hurting. I wondered where my last bottle of Jack was. I pulled back what was left of the drapes. Outside the sky was silver and white. The river was kinda grey and sulking, her banks were the color of cigarette ash. There was a nice little spot down there — my own private bar — underneath an old willow tree, where the sand was dry and white and where a girl could watch the river go by. Sitting and wondering if those waters could wash away her sins, or drown her? Maybe it could do both. I needed to feel my toes in the cold embrace of that big old water. I needed my mouth round a bottle of something real strong.

The Old Woman and the River

The old woman sits on her wicker chair and watches the Missouri slough past. That beautiful big old river. Thinking about those days does her no good. No good at all. Shame is a tough stain to cleanse from your heart. Maybe it's the toughest. Oh, there was guilt too. Another bastard to remove. And guilt was a stain she'd always done real well.

So, instead of thinking, the woman spends her days doing time with a great American river, as she runs the last forty miles, before a confluence with her big brother at St Louis. Dry times these days. Dry because they have to be. And she has to be. She reminds herself that every minute a woman lives — every minute beyond the point she should have drowned — needs to be quality time. She knows that river will keep on flowing, like it does every morning and every evening, day after day. Always flowing. Like life. It reminds the woman how long thirty years really is. It gets her thinking again.

A girl becomes a woman.

A woman becomes an object.

An object goes under, but refuses to drown.

A woman can grow old before her time.

A whole new take on the circle of life…

There are no mirrors in the woman's house anymore. Every pane of glass is shrouded by curtains or drapes or window shutters. When she takes an afternoon walk, it's always a few steps away from the river. There are no reflections in her world. No reminders. In her heart — and for as long as she wants — she can still be that young Cherokee woman, with her high golden cheeks, her eyes wide and dark and her hair black and shining like Melanite. She can still be the goddess with the body that drove men to their knees. And in her honest moments, she can remind herself that fifty-three isn't really that old — unless you've tried to squeeze too much into those years.

The great river moves a lot slower now, like the woman does. So maybe the Missouri's grown old before her time as well. She's turned the color of a drought — deep grey-green. It hasn't rained in the heart-land — not properly, not the way it once did — for a long time. There are people in this little town who have never seen the great river in flood. They're building dream houses right on the banks. The town neglects her levees. These people don't know about danger — about stuff. The older souls know things. Souls that live inside the old woman and the river.

They know…

ARCHIE

I remember another day — another fist knocking. This time it was a gentler rap. A rap from another soul. I was balled in the chaos of my little bed, almost naked, lying under a stained white bath towel that smelled like whiskey and unwashed man ... again.

'What this time?'

Reality began slapping me, though not hard enough to properly remember. Something was wrong. Part of the story was lost. It felt like a part I really should have remembered. I sat up, unhinging the towel and the pain in my temples. Nausea surged a warm gasping evil. I took deep breaths. Closed my eyes. Survived. You get better at doing the morning after, when it's every-other-day.

So who had it been this time?

I slid back the moldy curtains to see if the world was the same — grass, cliffs, trees, sky — if the river was still flowing. I hadn't drowned. Hadn't been cleansed of my sins. I was high and dry, and still at the Reach. It'd been raining. Low silver clouds like spirits, floating silently over the river. The world was wet and still and grey. For a moment I was almost OK. There was a precious morsel of peace. And then the knocking started again.

'Hello?'

It was another man's voice. An older man. It wasn't one of "them." His was a voice I knew; a throat that might have been full of razors; a rasping sing-song melody. And I knew he wouldn't go away.

'Is everything alright in there? Hello...'

'Yeah.' I barked, sounding like some beat-up Chandelle stray. 'Yeah, I'm fine.'

But then the nausea swam back. Flushing hot then cold. Head melting. My mouth full of car keys. I was so thirsty.

'Well, OK. I'll be right next door if you need anything.'

I lay back down. Closed my eyes. And I spent a few hours trying not to drown.

It was late afternoon before I was strong enough to face the world. The rain had passed and the sky was blue and white and grey. Cool breeze through my broken glass. I went searching around the trailer, put on some slightly fresher clothes, found an orphaned cigarette, lit up, and walked outside.

My neighbor was kneeling down, plucking weeds and humming a tune. This was George Washington

Archer Jnr — Archie — my morning visitor. A skin and bones man, with a face like a melted action figure, eyebrows like escaped rodents and huge iced-coffee eyes. He wore his curly white hair too long, almost shoulder length, with long wispy sideburns and a fringe combed backwards, like he'd been riding a motorbike without a helmet. I watched him for a few seconds, noticing the joy he received from doing something as simple as gardening.

How did you do that? Achieve that sense of peace?

My smoke drifted towards him. He turned, struggled to his feet and dusted wet earth from his hands straight onto the back of his baggy green shorts. He wore those shorts too high on his stomach. His legs were grey-brown and set wide apart. He had funny little round kneecaps — creases like eyes and a mouth — like they had faces.

'Oh hello there,' he croaked, flashing a woody yellow smile.

'Hi.'

'How are you feeling?'

'I'm OK.'

'Oh good. I was so worried about you after last night.'

He smiled again, the afternoon sun burning crevices across his dark face.

'So did you take me inside? Put me in bed?'

'I didn't want to leave you out there. There was rain coming. You didn't look very well. So I carried you back into your trailer and made sure you were safe.'

'I was drunk and half-naked.'

'Yes. I remember. I did wonder why you were down there like that. But not my business…'

I didn't know what to think. He must have seen me lying there, in just a bra and panties, down on the bank of the river, with an empty bottle of whiskey beside me. I remember sitting on the sand, with my toes in the water and getting wasted. Thinking how easy it would be to wade on in and drown. But Archie found me first, picked me up, probably held me close, and lifted me inside. What did he see? What did he do? He could have done anything.

He looked at me with those big crazy brown eyes of his. 'Yes, I know…' he said. 'A pretty girl, passed out, in just her underwear…'

He obviously read minds.

'…well, a man'd be crazy not to get to thinking… you know… be tempted to…'

'Were you?'

'No. So I must be crazy.'

That smile again. Wider. I noticed some of his teeth were missing.

'Maybe God was watching,' I said, trying to be funny. Not thinking.

'Maybe. What do you think?'

'Oh, I don't know. Me and God ain't exactly on speaking terms.'

I took a last puff on my cigarette and crushed it under the heel of my old trainer. Archie stared, smiling the whole time. There was dancing in his eyes and I wasn't sure what to believe.

I'd known him for a few months — the length of time I'd been at the Reach. He was a Baptist preacher, dethroned, defrocked, or whatever they call it. Fired. There were rumors — screwing members of his flock was the favorite — but then there'd been last night. He told me he didn't do anything and as I looked into his eyes for a second time, I knew I believed him. And I knew he'd been done wrong, by the church or by God or by everyone. I just knew. I'd have called it woman's intuition, if I believed in that stuff.

'Feel like shooting the breeze?' he asked, waddling over to the front of his trailer and picking up an ancient folding chair.

It was exactly the same as the chair my father used to sit on back home in Chandelle. He'd sit out back, staring at the weeds and all his piles of junk, and he'd drink beers with my older brother and they'd get wasted. If he got completely hammered, he'd spend the night outside, sleeping in the dirt with the rattle snakes. Sometimes though, he'd be sober enough to make it back into the house. And then he'd come looking for me…

'No,' I stuttered. 'I mean not…'

'That's OK, I'll just blabber to myself then.'

He unfolded his chair in the narrow green space between our two trailers, sat and stared out onto the river. A pair of brown ducks came flying overhead, dropping, landing and sliding long white cuts along the river. Then they slid together as a pair. I could hear their soft quacking sounds.

'Beautiful…' Archie said.

Suddenly I didn't want to go inside. I sat on the grass beside Archie's chair and waited for something, for anything, to happen.

'I love it here,' he whispered, like he knew I was going to stay. 'And I figure if I stay here long enough, I might convince someone to rename this Archie's Reach.'

'You're joking?'

'No ma'am. This is heaven to me. Where else in the world can you live on a beautiful river front for only fifteen dollars a week?'

'Yeah, in a busted up trailer.'

'Inside the ugliest oyster grows the most beautiful pearl…'

'Huh…?' I began to regret not going inside, if he was going to get all preachy on me.

It seemed like a long time before Archie spoke again.

'I remember when you first came here,' he said. 'When was that? A few months ago? I remember those two policemen, wearing cheap suits and mirror sunglasses. They were full of tough talk and arrogance. I wondered what you'd done and why they were bringing you here. I wonder why they keep visiting you. And I wonder what your name is?'

'Lisa,' I said, feeling guilty. 'Lisa Hewson.'

'Lisa. Lovely Lisa,' he said, almost musically.

I didn't reply.

'So, why are you here Lisa?'

'I could ask you the same thing.'

'And I'd be pleased to tell you, if you have a little time on your hands.'

I did. I had forever.

He turned to me and smiled. Showed those funny yellow teeth of his. 'OK,' he said; 'hang on.'

I crossed my legs, sat with my hands on my knees, like we used to back in Elementary School when it was story time.

'There's a thing about church folk that they don't tell you in the brochures,' he said. 'Well, they never told me. Or maybe I was just some naïve little black boy, fresh out of bible school. But see, I could never stand back while folks in the community were hurting,

and watch the church pour money into stuff we
didn't need.'

'What sort of stuff?' I asked.

'Silly things, like new musical instruments when we
had perfectly adequate old ones. Fancy P.A systems,
when all we really needed was a few good loud voices.
Ornaments of crystal and gold. These things were very
important to the folks where I was Pastor, Lisa.'

He grunted and looked at me, perhaps wondering
what I might say. I just shrugged.

'Yes, well, these people built this church. I mean
actually built it, with their own hands and money. They
were real proud of their little church and the things
they'd achieved. I told them they were right to feel
happy with what they'd made, but that it was time
for a new priority. Time to give back. Time to listen
to what God might have been saying to them. Now,
you need to understand, this was in Willow Hills. I
don't know if you've ever heard of this place. It's just
outside Dallas. Well, we had some real big issues in
that community. Lots of crime. Kids skipping school.
Unemployment. Homelessness. Drugs and booze. Lisa,
I never understood how there could be so many people
in the world who have so little, when our world has so
much. Y'know?'

I nodded. I sure did.

'So we had families in our neighborhood, really doing it tough. Latino families. White families. Black families. Refugees from Vietnam and Cambodia. They needed help. I asked the congregation for some money ... the money they'd saved up for some more church improvements ... to give to these families.'

'And they kicked you out for asking?'

'No, they kicked me out when they said no, but I went ahead and spent the money anyway. They accused me of stealing. I mean, I guess I did, but it felt like we had been stealing from God all along. I mean, these folks would tell you all good things came from God. Lisa, they'd say it to your face. But if you wanted to use money to help their brothers and sisters in the community ... well, suddenly it was their money.' He leaned back in his chair. Exhaled loudly. 'But I must say, they were very fair. They told me I could quit and leave town, or they'd call the police and charge me with theft.'

'You shitting me?' I snorted. 'Sorry, I mean, really?'

'Yes, really. So what could I do? I resigned. It was tough to leave. We'd made some beautiful friends at that church. But work wise, you know, it was no big deal. I expected to pick up a position in another parish. There were always churches looking for an experienced Pastor. But I didn't anticipate the reach of some of my flock.

The lengths they would go to, you know, to denigrate my name. No one would have me in their church after that. And then Edna fell ill.'

'Your wife?'

'Not only my wife.' He paused for a second. Looked at the grass. Smiled to himself. 'Lisa, have you ever really been hopelessly in love with someone? I mean, really hopeless ... to the point where you can't really function with or without them?'

I started studying the grass too. Honesty burning. Suddenly ashamed. 'No, I haven't.'

'Well, God willing you will ... one day. Anyway, that was how I felt about my Edna. We met in Fort Worth just after the war. Oh, you should have seen her that night Lisa, her eyes like honeycomb, and a dress that was the color of the ocean. I couldn't breathe. She was so beautiful.' He was quiet again. Gave a little snort. 'Two months and boom, we were married. We owned nothing. We had no grand plans. We just had each other. This sounds stupid, I know, but it was like I hadn't really been able to breathe until I met Edna. She switched on my heart.'

'What happened?' I asked.

'Cancer. Edna and I could never have children and the doctors never really knew why ... at least the doctors we could afford to visit. She started having pains in her 40's and they always put it down to stomach flu or irritated bowel or something. But it wasn't. And by the time we found out, well…'

He fell silent. The wind began blowing through my hair. A warm wind, but I felt so cold. You can't imagine how much hate I had inside me…

'Ovarian cancer is a terrible thing, Lisa. It's like a thief in the night. By the time you know it's there, it's usually too late. So, in a year, I lost my job and then I lost my wife. That's kind of rough on a man.'

'So you came here?'

'No, not straight away. I worked for a soup kitchen in Dallas, serving food to the homeless. I did some prison work for a while. Counseling. Chaplaincy. I managed to save enough money to buy a trailer and go traveling. I didn't travel too far. As soon as I found this place, I knew this was where I'd stay. And now … here I am … talking to you.'

'You never considered another wife?'

'My wife's with her Lord, Lisa.'

'I guess, but…'

'Edna's buried over in Fort Worth, with her folks. I couldn't afford a plot, so I managed to pay for her to be cremated and her ashes were put with her mom's. I mean, I guess they are. I've never been brave enough to go back and see. That was fifteen years ago Lisa. And

I've never felt the need to marry again. I don't think it's in God's plan.'

'So you still believe in God,' I said, kinda amazed. 'After all that, you still believe in God?'

'Amazing huh.'

'That's one word for it.'

'Bad things happen Lisa. Real bad things, sometimes. But I can't be sad about what I've been through, 'cause I've made plenty of mistakes and I've suffered the consequences. And I've been wonderfully blessed too. That's life. God doesn't do these things to us, we bring it on ourselves. Do you understand?'

'Yuh,' I replied. 'Believe it or not, yeah I understand exactly.'

I'd run away from home fifteen years ago. The same year Archie's wife died. That was the first time. I went home again. Who runs away when they're only eight? It took me another nine years to do it for real. I'd brought plenty on myself too. I wondered if I'd ever have the guts to tell him.

Eventually Archie and I had to say goodnight. We went inside to escape the bugs. I staggered back to my trailer and stood, alone and numb, in the yellow glow of my last light bulb. I stared at my reflection in the wardrobe mirror, and hated. I hated myself. Hated those people who did Archie wrong. Why him? It can't have just been the church money. Was it racial? Hell, of course it was. Man, I hated them even more. And I hated God most of all — 'cause deep down he coulda stopped it. Couldn't he?

He coulda stopped everything bad in the world.

As the evening rain swept in, lashed the windows and leaked through my broken glass, I slumped at the foot of my bed, wrapped myself around a new bottle of Tennessee gold, and drank. I cried my eyes out. And then drank some more. I tried my hardest to drown again.

It was a week until I next saw Archie. He vanished, without a word of explanation as to where he was going. I started drowning in loneliness. I don't think I'd ever experienced anything quite like that feeling. I spent the week locked away from the rain, swallowing painkillers with bourbon.

I had another visit from the rookie cop with the orange tan. He wanted a blowjob this time, but I told him to go to hell. I jerked him off again. Then, once he'd gone, I took a razor-blade out of my shaver, sat on my bed and cut his initials into my forearm. And, even as the blade buried into my skin and those scarlet letters wept onto the floor, I wondered why I couldn't feel any pain.

It was a moist honey-colored morning and, as I lay sun-burning beside my trailer, Archie came back. I'd been lying on the grass for about an hour, when I heard his folding chair click open and there he was, sitting beside me like he'd never left. It felt good to have him back, but I didn't really understand why.

'So, what do you think?' he said, lifting up his straw grandpa hat and showing me his new haircut.

'Great,' I replied, turning around to have a look. I mean, it was OK, just a standard haircut. But I thought he was still wearing it way too long for his age.

'Oh yes. Had this done while I was up in Sioux, which is where all the guys in my family get their hair cut. Pablo the hair guy, Lisa. Bit of a genius in my book.'

I grunted and lay back down on my towel. He was a funny old guy. And what a pair we must have made, me sun-baking in my red bikini and Archie, sitting hunched in long baggy shorts, a white cotton singlet and his new haircut under that straw grandpa hat. Perhaps he was an old man keeping watch over a wayward granddaughter. Or something like that...

'You know Lisa,' he said after a few minutes silence. 'I often wonder.'

'About what?'

I looked up at him. He was staring over to the other side of the Reach. Staring at cliffs of the brightest yellow and orange and gold; cliffs burning against the blue of the day. Most of the land over there had been cleared for pasture, but there were still groves of birch and pine, down in the valleys, where tiny creeks trickled like ice water, to join the slow surge of the Missouri.

'About what it must have been like for the Sioux, watching from up there, while the white men came and cleared the river flats and took their land. How must they have felt?'

'I dunno. I'm Cherokee. My people came from the Carolinas. I don't know much about it. My folks never talked about our people. I guess it was bad for them. It's bad for all of us. But the white folks did your people wrong as…'

'…to see something so beautiful ripped apart and ruined and not being able to do anything to stop it. The injustice of that.'

'Do you want me to say something?' I asked, retying my bikini top, sitting up, and wondering why he was bothering me with this.

He didn't reply. He just kept staring at those cliffs.

A small wooden boat came chugging into the Reach, pushing into the twists and eddies of the surging current. There was a big pink-colored guy onboard, dressed in a white shirt and green fishing pants, leaning forward, like he was willing his craft on. Archie stared at the boat, eyes wide and fascinated, like it was the most important thing he'd seen in his life. Waiting. In no hurry to continue our conversation.

Only when the air fell silent again, did he speak; 'Do you?'

'Do I what?'

'Want to tell me something?'

'About being Native American? About injustice?'

'About that … or anything else?'

I looked up at the sky, bright blue and dripping with humidity; at those tiny fragments of undisturbed forest; the injustice of this life. I felt my heart tearing apart.

The things I had done.

The bad decisions.

The attempts at drowning.

I knew he knew. He was just waiting for me to tell him. Listening to my stories was the most important thing in his life at that moment. I knew that.

'I want to tell you about everything,' I finally whispered.

'Well, you know, I'd like that. So let's make it soon.'

And with that, he packed up his chair and wandered back to his trailer.

I lay there, paralyzed and bleeding. In a few words, he'd found me. Cut me deeper than any blade. I couldn't leave it at that. I wanted to crawl back into the dark, dive into another bottle — and drink and drink and drink. But I couldn't. Not this time. It was time to get it all out there. It was time to talk. So this time I went after him.

Archie didn't invite me inside, but I went in anyway. His trailer was the same size as mine, but a world apart. The interior was neatly cluttered, shelves jammed tight with a rainbow of book spines. Every flat surface held something. Even his spare bed was buried under papers and files and folders. He had two picture frames on the wall above his bed: Dr King in one and a beautiful, smiling girl in the other. I guessed it was his late-wife. The air was a strange mix of cleaning products and dust. His world was spotless and filthy together. It was almost as big a mystery as he was.

He was still in the singlet and shorts, but the hat was gone. I'd done my hair and slipped a mini-dress over my bikini. My back and arms were stinging from the sunburn. I was parched and nervous. I wanted to run away. Instead, I sat down and waited for him to say something.

'Coffee?' his back eventually asked.

'Thanks, cream and two sugars.'

'Well wouldn't you know … exactly the same as me!'

He turned and smiled, and I just knew he'd planned to make his coffee the same way as mine, no matter how that was. He was just waiting for me to tell him.

Oh, I know it's stupid, but that did it for me. A silent tear fell, as the first drops of rain began to fall on the roof of his trailer. Unfamiliar warmth filled my chest.

And I smiled. At that moment, and for the first time in my life, I fell hopelessly in love with someone. I mean love, not lust or dependence or some sort of dumb longing. Love — like I'd do anything for him and like I just knew he'd do anything for me. My God, he was probably three times my age, but the feelings I had for Archie at that moment…

We sat for hours — devouring three cups of coffee and some stale cinnamon cake — and I told Archie everything. I didn't stop. Above the constant drumming of the heaviest rain I can remember, I told him my stories. I told him about growing up in Texas — in that shit hole, Chandelle — and about my useless family. I told him how my dad used to beat up mom when he'd had too much to drink. How he'd whip on me and my two brothers if we said anything to try and make the beating stop. And how my brother Jerry got murdered when someone messed with the brakes on his car, but how the cops didn't investigate it, because it was our family … and when it came to the law, our family didn't count for shit. We were just another no good bunch of half-caste Injuns, spooning off the government and causing trouble. It wasn't true, but that's what folks thought.

I told Archie how I rebelled and ran away to Chicago when it all got too much. Even though I was good at school — and might have even made it to college — I gave it all up and ran. God, I was only seventeen. I told him about my six years of drink and drugs and working the streets. And yes, I hooked up with the wrong people, and I did some terrible — shameful — things. I told Archie this. They were clichéd stories, but they were true. And they were mine. I closed my eyes, and…

…I remembered the last time. I started to tell Archie about it. There'd been a big bust by the Vice Squad in Chicago. That was the last time alright. I'd been living with a leather-clad giant called Tyrone — though most of the cats called him Buff, short for Big Ugly Fat Fighter, which wasn't the exact translation, but I didn't like swearing in front of Archie — and I'd been hustling for him for about a year. A little place off North Rush. Another near the lakefront. Buff was always moving. Always trying to stay a step ahead of the cops.

It was early on a Saturday morning when the cops hunted him down. I'd been with Buff and some of his dudes that night. Bad cats. A long dirty Friday night — speedballs and gang rape — that left me collapsed on the lounge floor, with a towel over me. All I could remember was a busted ass and a stinking towel. It was about six in the morning when the door was kicked in. Buff was long gone. They all were. Buff had ears in the cops. He found out they were coming about the same time they did. But he never thought of telling me. I'd passed my sell-by date. I was expendable. Sacrificed — 'cause cops always liked to get a body when they made a bust. The first thing I remember was being pushed against a wall, off my face and still nude, while a female officer put on a glove and stuck two fingers up me, looking for jacks. And then she totally freaked out when she saw the state of my asshole. She insisted on calling the paramedics.

Can you believe I told all these things to Archie?

After I was cleared by the paramedics, the cops took me down to 103rd Street, locked me in a grey concrete cell. Left me there. Yeah, I was healthy enough, so they put me in a cage. This was way into January. Cold as hell. They left me in that cell with just a smock and bare feet. I can never remember being that cold, before or since. The cops were torturing me — waiting for me to crack, so I'd roll over and talk. I tried screaming my head off, but they ignored me. Eventually, a short-hair dyke cop came over to my cell and told me the longer I kept screamin', the longer they would take. Told me she'd fix me up good and proper too. Oh man, I remember she licked her lips when she said it.

Eventually I was processed. The cops made me an offer I couldn't refuse. I wanted to get cleaned up. I wanted to go straight. I was freezing cold, and scared as hell. So I played ball. They got what they wanted. As part of the deal, I ratted on Buff and his pals.

Turns out, good old Buff had form all over the U.S. He had about twenty aliases and was wanted under each of them. The FBI became involved. And the DEA. They all wanted me to testify, so they put me under witness protection. The city paid for me to clean up and sent me to a refuge out in Oak Park. Then, once I was clean, the Feds started putting me into safe houses: Chicago, then St Louis, Oklahoma City, some little shit-hole in Iowa. South Dakota — The Reach — was just the latest hiding place they'd tried. But Buff always found me. I would call 911 and hope the cavalry got to me before Buff did. They had so far, but I knew the good guys wouldn't always get there on time. And once I'd testified and my usefulness was over, I doubted they'd bother coming out for me at all. Buff would find me soon enough. And when he did find me, he was going to kill me. I told Archie about that too.

I opened my eyes again. I felt breathless and so very cold. It was like being in that grey cell again. Archie was holding his coffee cup, eyes wide, just listening. There was no scowl of judgment, no head-shaking pity. He nodded quietly.

'I'm so sorry, Archie,' I said, my fingers shaking.

'For?'

'For unloading all that stuff on you. I mean, you must really think I'm some piece of work, y'know, now that you know the things I've done. Well…' my hands really started shaking. I couldn't stop them, even if I held onto them tight. I could feel tears start to burn. '…go ahead. Give me a sermon.'

Archie didn't reply. He began making swirls in the dust of the table with the fingers of his right hand. Closed his eyes. Outside the rain eased and then stopped altogether. There was an unearthly silence. Clouds parting. I could see the milky glow of a freshly washed moonlight through the drapes. Or was it something else? Still, Archie said nothing.

'No sermon, Lisa,' he finally whispered. 'There is no one in this room so without transgression that they be qualified for finger-waving. No one here is entitled to hurl sinless stones.' He looked up from the table and smiled. 'But I would like to say thank you.'

'Thank you, for what?'

'For having the courage to share your story.' He reached forward, took my right hand in his, lifted it to his face, and kissed it.

Suddenly, both hands stopped shaking. The warm glow in my chest again. And outside, the land seemed to be ablaze with moonlight.

'And thank you for sharing it with me,' Archie said. 'It's a privilege when someone shares their heart with another person. Too many folks don't do that, and our world is poorer as a result. If more of us shared our stories, perhaps we'd learn to bend a little more and break a little less. So, yes Lisa, thank you.'

I got to my feet and stumbled around the table to him. I kinda fell into his arms. We hugged. There were sobs and tears—from both of us. It took me a long time before I felt strong enough to let him go. We both sat back in our seats.

'OK,' he said. 'I want you to promise me something.'

'I'll try.'

'I want you to promise that if you're ever in trouble—with this Tyrone Buff person or the police or anyone else—then I want you to tell me and I want you to ask for my help.' He took my hand again. Gave it a little shake. 'Will you promise me this Lisa?'

'Sure,' I replied, wondering if I would.

Outside, the luminosity faded into darkness and raindrops began to fall once more. I wondered what the hell someone like Archie could do against the police, or, worse still, a dangerous bastard like Buff. Thunder above the trailer. And I began to worry that I might not have long to wait until I found out.

Archie's Reach

It took six months. The man everyone knew as Buff followed another trail of bribes and threats until he finally found my little corner of the world. He found me at the Reach, just as he had found me everywhere else.

I'd been dreaming—something about my mom and moving with her over to the Carolinas where the weather was warm and where we could start again. We had…

And then I woke to the sound of a car door slamming. I sat up in bed. I slid a crack in the curtains, wondering which cop had arrived this time, and what they were going to expect from me. After talking with Archie, I was determined that the cop favors would stop as well. I had started to be strong and stand up for myself. For the first time, in as long as I could remember, I was standing up for what was right.

But this wasn't a cop. This was…

I shivered. The air sucked from my chest.

'Oh no, no no no no no…'

He hadn't changed since I'd last seen him: same crappy black Mustang; same cut-up jeans and torn white t-shirt; same fraying brown leather jacket; his hair still a giant helmet of tight black curls, like a Motown singer. He stood beside the car for a moment, stretched both arms above his head and yawned, like he had all the time in the world, like a man without an enemy on the earth, or like a man who knew exactly what he wanted. He wanted me. I watched as he started walking towards the door of my trailer.

I dropped back the curtain, wallowed down into the bed clothes, and froze. I listened to his footsteps on the damp earth. Slow and heavy. His clicking fingers. A familiar rhythm. Sounds I'd come to fear.

There was the scuff of his boot on the concrete block outside my door.

There was his voice roaring outside the trailer.

There was the sound of him bouncing off the river.

God help me.

Surely, now, it was over.

He began attacking the door with his feet and his fists. From down in my bed, I could see cracks of light forming around the frame. I could see the tips of his fingers reaching around the edges. It'd only taken him seconds and he was almost inside…

'Open the door Lisa,' he roared. 'I'm gonna kick the mother in, so you betta just open it … save me gettin' real mad.'

I caught a glimpse of him — a dark snapshot against the frame of morning glare. I saw the silver mirror of his shades, the golden gleam of his two front teeth, those thick brown and pink lips. I saw the rings on his fingers as he reached inside to try and unlatch the door, the scarring on his right hand where a rival's blade had once cut him. I could hear the wet heaving of his breath as he struggled to break inside. A sound so familiar to me, usually coming from behind, when he was…

And then, suddenly, he moved away from the door. There was a bright flash of morning as his shadow disappeared. I heard another voice. A little sing-song voice. A voice crackling and happy.

'Can I help you with anything?' I heard Archie ask.

'Who the hell are you?'

I crawled out of bed, slid across to the other side of the trailer and peered under the blinds. Archie was standing a few feet away from Buff, in his baggy green shorts, an old blue shirt, and that silly straw grandpa hat. He was smiling away, yellow picket fence teeth, puppet eyes wide and happy looking. He looked like a man without a problem in the world.

'I'm a friend,' Archie said, offering his hand.

'How about you get yo'self lost old man, while you can.'

'Now … now, let's try and keep it friendly shall we.'

'Say what?'

'You're Tyrone I suspect. Now I don't think you're supposed to be here … are you? So here's what I think you should do.'

Buff moved towards Archie; a predator ready to strike. 'I think you better shut your mouth brother. While you still can.'

Archie didn't move. He slid his hands into his pockets and kept on politely smiling, like the two of them were discussing the garden.

'Come on, I think it might be better if you just left, don't you?'

'What the fuck?'

'Look, there's nothing for you here, so please just leave. If you hop in your car now and go, before the police arrive, we promise we won't say a word to them about you being here. Go off and live your life. Start again. Just leave, please Tyrone. C'mon my friend, just let it end…'

There was that roaring sound again. I knew it well. I wanted to cry out, to tell Archie to stop. I watched as Buff began to bristle, muscles tensing, ready for the attack. Archie must have seen it too, but he didn't flinch. That stupid little man was determined to protect me.

'Tyrone, I'm really sorry,' Archie muttered, shaking his head and walking away, 'If you won't…' I thought I heard him say the word "police…"

He was still shaking his head when the two of them came together. I watched as his legs were sent flying—as a small man was consumed by a giant. A scream sat in my throat, hissing and scratching like a wild cat, but refusing to leave. It happened too quickly after that. A blade flashed, like a camera bulb. A hint of death. Punching jabs. And then I saw Archie roll out of leather arms and collapse onto the grass. His arms started flapping at his side. I saw Buff give him a kick in the head. Another. Archie's face rolled into the grass and his arms stopped flailing. Then Buff turned and ran towards my trailer again.

'Open the door bitch,' he shrieked. 'Your turn.'

I can't really explain what happened next. I don't understand it fully myself. Something inside me boiled. Flames that became sounds. The cry of a devil, or worse.

I screamed—no, it was much more than a scream— and I didn't stop until I heard his car door slam and the sound of his tires spinning on gravel. I screamed as I ran all the way down Freemason Drive, to the phone booth, and I screamed at the 911 operator, until he threatened to have me locked up if I didn't stop yelling at him.

Nothing helped.

The paramedics had to come down from Springshore. It took them twenty minutes. Too long. Archie was almost gone by the time I got back to him. The front of his pale blue shirt was wet and purple. His face was bloody and broken. A fragment of tooth lay in a slick of bloody spit on his cheek. He was hardly moving. I fell down beside him, turned up his face and began whimpering to him.

'Please Archie. Please don't leave me.'

His left eye was already gone — swollen shut. His right eye met mine. Looking into that eye, I could see he was losing the battle to stay alive. He tried to speak, but no words came out. Bubbles of blood in his mouth. Another broken tooth floating in the mess.

'Archie. C'mon,' I begged. 'Stay alive. I've called 911. They're almost here. Stay alive Archie. I love you Archie. Please ... you have to know how much I love you. Please, stay alive for me.'

He slowly reached up and his hard cracked fingers touched my cheek. Archie's reach was warm and comforting and alive, even as his life slipped away.

'...member,' he whispered.

His hand dropped and I watched his eye go steely and lifeless. A shudder. And then another. He wasn't going to wait. He was leaving me. There was a last, horrible airless gasp and he was gone.

But then, deep in my heart, and just as his fell still, something unbelievable happened. I closed my eyes and I thought I heard him speak to me — one last time. He spoke a single word. It was clear and it was loud, and it was just for me...

'Grace.'

The Old Woman and Memories

As the old woman sits and stares at the water, she begins to remember what she cannot forget. The sight of leather and stainless steel. The awful metallic smell. A scarlet blight on fresh green grass. So much red. She hates the color red. She hates to remember the story. Is scared to forget.

A federal agent picked up the 911 call out to the paramedics, recognized the address and made a run for the trailer park. His cruiser caught Buff's Mustang coming out of Grey's Reach road. There was a brief gunfight. Residents across the river in Nebraska started making 911 calls to report shots fired.

When the Fire Department Paramedics arrived, they found a badly wounded Federal Agent and an unnamed black male deceased on Grey's Reach Road. They called for backup. They did what they could, but the agent couldn't be saved. In the end they took three bodies back to Springshore base. And all hell broke loose.

She remembers answering questions for three days straight. How they suddenly got serious about police protection and put her in that sleazy motor inn out near Springshore and posted a uniformed cop to guard her door, when it was all too late. She remembers how each day, another pair of pitbulls, in matching grey suits, would bang on her door, then sit her on the bed while they circled the room asking her the same stupid questions and trying to sneak a peek down her blouse. Different cops — same tactics. It must have been what they learnt at cop school or something. She told them everything she could remember. The same story: every … single … time. There was no point in lying — in making stuff up — not now.

The Buff was gone. He was out of her life. But then, so was Archie.

The woman doesn't like to think back too much. With some things, it would be better if you could forget. Still, she knows she needs to remember every once in a while. It reminds her how she managed to survive. And what her life came to cost. And still, after so many years, Lisa Hewson can't justify that price. Not for the likes of her. She finds it hard to believe that someone was prepared to jump in that river and drown in her place.

It didn't seem possible.

And on days like this, when the wind dies away and the river looks like raw glass, she remembers a warm smile, big puppet eyes and a happy sing-song voice. She remembers soft loving hands and the embrace of a man who knew what it really meant to love another person. She remembers how he reached out and stopped her from drowning. She remembers his word of grace.

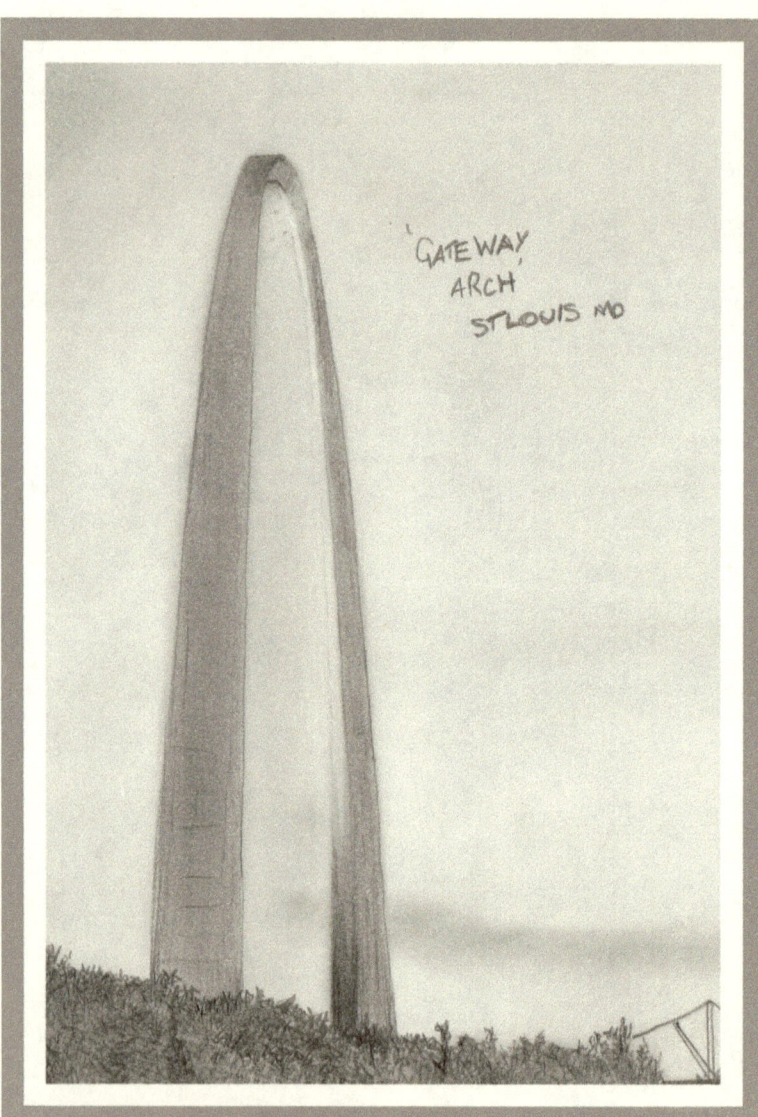

GATEWAY
ARCH
ST LOUIS MO

FIRST SNOW ... LAST

TODD JACKSON STOOD SO CLOSE TO THE WINDOW HIS breath began to fog the glass. Little opaque circles of breath ... appearing ... vanishing ... appearing...

...and again.

The sky was low and heavy, silver and grey, and he could see the first snow of the winter hovering over St Louis. It was just waiting for nightfall.

Everyone was.

Out to the east, beyond the red brick walls and dark green lawns of the university, beyond the beige office towers and the asphalt fingers of the I-40, Todd could see the tip of the Arch.

Gateway to the West.

Shining.

Shining.

He remembered those long lunches at *The Nest* bookstore, the angst of work, and that little voice he used to carry around in his head. A life when he was single and grumpy. A time poisoned for too long by regret.

But then he remembered the colors of the fall leaves in Gateway Park. The way they glittered like precious stones on the damp lawn. How all his worries about marrying late in life just faded when she arrived at his side. How they stood as one on a carpet of jade, surrounded by fields of rubies, beside an aquamarine lake. He remembered that fitted white dress and the shape of her. How her sharp Slavic features were made soft and angelic behind silk tulle. There was a smile that was just for him. Burning of tears, and the end of regret...

'Are you still there?' he heard her whisper.

'Yeah, of course.'

And he had been, for the last few nights and days. The hospital staff knew. He knew. The time was near. It was almost over. The concept of visiting hours no longer applied. They bent the rules — even brought in a folding cot for Todd to sleep on.

'I think that maybe it's going to snow tonight,' she said quietly, nodding towards the window. A smile on dry purple lips. She bled when she smiled.

So did he.

And he worried how many more smiles he would be allowed to see.

Todd reached gently for her hand. Hand without flesh. He felt the dry tissue of her skin, moving over bones like kindling. She shivered. Her wedding band swung on air. The injustice of losing her so soon—after so long alone. He'd spent so long wanting the girl he couldn't have. Wanting Sandra. But then there had been Katarina...

'I remember from my home,' he heard her whisper. 'The first snow was always the most beautiful.'

Then she closed her eyes. Slept. A face at peace.

You left me last night. Slipped away, silent, like the first flakes of winter. Nurse Walker woke me just after four. A soft touch on the arm to tell me it was over. My precious lady, you gave us all the slip. There wasn't a sound. You left with such grace and such silent poise. It wasn't ugly and it wasn't beautiful, it was private and it was personal. It was just between you and the Lord. You always told me you wanted it that way.

The snow lay thick on the ground outside. Dawn's waxy glare gave light to a room no longer occupied. A room devoid of soul. They gave me a few minutes alone with you. I kissed your forehead. Familiar skin now cold. That's when I knew you had gone, and I believed you'd gone to someplace better. No point lingering. I called them back to the room and they took your body away.

That was when the nurse gave me your note, as I was packing up our things. They found it in the pocket of your night dress. No one knows when you wrote it. Or how? You never asked for a pen. You had no paper. Your written English was never great. And your hands would shake so much you couldn't hold a pen, let alone write. Yet there it was, in clear, crisp words:

"I have to leave you tonight Todd. It has only been three years, I know, but they were three wonderful years. The best years of my life. Don't let this upset you, my darling. It is time. Time to move on. You trust in God, don't you? Then be still and believe. There is room for all in the house of our Father. Room for me and room for you. Room for all who believe. So now I am on my way. I'll be waiting for you. Waiting as patiently for you — just as you waited for me. You spent so many years alone — and now you must be alone again. But it won't be forever. So rest and know that I am at peace. I am home. Rest and know I will always be with you. Now and for eternity. Yours always, Katarina."

I folded the paper and put it in the pocket of my coat. No tears now. I felt you with me in that room again. I felt the weight of your love — lifting my burden. Even in death, it felt like you were guiding my way and keeping me safe. How typical of you, my love. You always cared about others more than yourself.

With you, it was always about other folks.

MORE BOOKS

AIDEN'S ALIBI

A year into mourning his wife, James Davison still wonders how to move on. Could Aiden's mother be the answer, or just another question? Is this the real thing, or something else altogether? James's life is about to get a lot more complicated.

This brilliant contemporary story of love, lust and loss is Book One in D.B Allen's Modern Relationships Series, and is followed by Book Two, The Rainbow Blindness..

by D.B. ALLEN

THE RAINBOW BLINDNESS

What do you do when you discover you're not the person everyone thought you should be? Your parents. Your friends. Your town. How can you be yourself, when you don't understand who you are? And how do you describe the beauty of a rainbow, when you're the only person who can see it? The Rainbow Blindness is a story about self-discovery, love and loathing, set against a background of great beauty and looming darkness.

ABOUT THE AUTHOR

D.B. Allen writes contemporary stories about human relationships in our complex modern world. He is passionate about characters and spirit, as well as landscape and the way our environment helps define who we are.

DB's debut novella, Aiden's Alibi, was published by Silky Oak Press in late 2013, and was followed up by a second novella, The Rainbow Blindness.

Heart Land is his first full length novel.

www.ingramcontent.com/pod-product-compliance
Lightning Source LLC
Chambersburg PA
CBHW051242250626
47155CB00009B/3132